A SCANDAL BEFORE CHRISTMAS

APRIL MORAN

A SCANDAL BEFORE CHRISTMAS

By
April Moran

A Scandal Before Christmas

Cover designed by: Dragonfly Ink Graphic Design

Editing by: Kendra's Editing and Book Services

www.kendragaither.com

For James
Always

A SPRIG OF MISTLETOE

Beneath a sprig of mistletoe
I found my love.
And stole from those lips
The beat of my heart.
Only to return it
A thousand times o'er.
A thousand wicked kisses
Just before Christmas
At the stroke of midnight.

CHAPTER 1

LADY LAUREN GEORGIANNA KENDALL considered returning to London as the coach trudged along. But it had taken almost forty-eight hours to come this far, and she was close to her destination.

It was so cold. No, it was more than that. It was positively freezing, the wind cutting with such sharp bitterness, she wondered how anyone could stand it.

A loud snap of the reins reminded Lauren of the driver handling the coach in such foul weather. Sympathy flashed through her. She hoped his coat, and that of the horses, too, proved thick enough to withstand the biting wind.

Yesterday, it had taken only a few hours on the train to travel from London to the tiny town of Farringdon. The train's passenger car was relatively luxurious, with emerald colored seats and brass lanterns. Lauren's maid, Anne, sat with her while

Ollie, Lord Kendall's former manservant, traveled in a separate area along with other male servants. Anne practically bounced on the richly hued velvet, excited by her first train ride.

Debarking in Farringdon for the next leg of the trip, Lauren immediately hired this coach upon the train master's recommendation. But the four-in-hand vehicle, jostling over the ruts and holes in the road, was certainly a reminder of more primitive travel. Snowdrifts impeded their progress, stretching the time it would normally take to reach Settleton Hall in Stratford. For the safety of the driver and the horses, they'd spent the previous night at a cozy inn along the way.

Turning back for London was not an option at this point. Viscount and Viscountess Settleton were expecting her, and besides, Mother would not allow her cousin's invitation to be declined anyway. She insisted Lauren go, even if it meant going alone.

"I hope Lady Kendall is feeling better." Anne snuggled under the carriage blanket, propping her boots beside Lauren's on the tin can of coals keeping the coach's interior on the edge of being warm. On the opposite seat, Ollie was fast asleep, wedged upright in the corner. The man would have ridden up top with the driver, but because he'd nearly frozen to death the day before, Lauren insisted he ride inside the coach today.

"Mrs. Townsend is taking excellent care of her," Lauren replied. In fact, their housekeeper treated Lady Kendall as if she were the Queen herself.

Her mother was recuperating from a recent illness. She could not travel with the bitterly cold weather currently gripping England.

When Lauren said she would remain home and continue caring for her, Mother objected at once.

"No, you simply mustn't miss it, Lauren," her mother claimed in an almost panicked tone.

Lauren swallowed the lump of guilt rising in her throat.

She'd spent a year mourning her father's death. But when the opportunity presented itself, she readily escaped London. Did that make her a terrible daughter? The fact she was so eager to experience gaiety and laughter again? Even with her mother's blessing, she wondered if she was doing the right thing.

Lauren's jaw tightened. She could, and would, venture out into society. She was her own woman now, responsible for herself and her decisions. There was only one person to whom she would have answered, had matters progressed as planned.

Fisting the coach blanket in agitation, she told herself she would not think of "*that day.*"

But that was impossible.

The call had not been a pleasant one. Just a week following her father's funeral, Lauren faced her betrothed. There, in the drawing room of her parents' Mayfair home, she broke off her engagement with the man who had stolen her heart.

Even now, her heart clenched painfully at the memory.

"It's good you decided to go to Stratford, milady. You deserve a chance to make merry," Anne said, her teeth chattering. "Although I do wish it were warmer."

"I do as well," Lauren agreed softly, pulled from her memories. "We should be there soon, I think."

It wasn't much longer that a knock on the coach roof alerted them of their imminent arrival at their destination.

Ollie sat up with a start while Anne giggled.

"Have we arrived, milady?" He removed his spectacles, blinking like an owl at the two women.

"It appears we have." Lauren adjusted her cloak, lifting the coach's small window curtain to see the house come into view down a long, tree-lined drive. She pretended not to see the wink the servant gave her maid. She was well aware of the budding romance between the two of them and thought it quite sweet.

Accepting the coachman's hand as she descended the coach

steps, Lauren was immediately bundled within an oversized blanket of blue tartan. It must have been warmed by the fire, for it was toasty, smelling of chestnuts and cinnamon. She inhaled the scent with appreciation while tucking her hands within her ermine muff.

"Let's get you out of this wind, my dear," George, her cousin's husband, stated cheerfully. The viscount pulled Lauren along, his larger form blocking the stronger winds as they hurried up the manor's steps. Behind them, servants helped Anne and Ollie with the baggage.

Several guests were gathered in the large foyer, and in the midst of the merry confusion, Lauren was warmly embraced by her cousin, Penelope.

"My dear Lauren, it is wonderful to see you after so many months. We've been so worried for your arrival with the temperamental weather." The viscountess squeezed Lauren tight then held her away so she could better look her over. "Still as lovely as ever, but you are too thin. No worries, though. We shall remedy that well enough over the next few weeks."

Lauren grinned, gratified that marriage apparently agreed with Penelope. Her cousin's face still glowed as it had after her wedding to the earl just two years before.

"I see you still like to meddle," Lauren teased.

"Guilty, I'm afraid." A spark of something lit Penelope's soft blue eyes. "I hope you forgive me for it, too."

"How can I not? Thank you for inviting me for Christmas. I'm so sorry Mother could not accompany me."

"I do hope she is feeling better. I'm sure the past few months have been very difficult."

Lauren nodded as the chatter around them ebbed and flowed. Her cousin must have invited nearly two dozen people to spend the holidays at Settleton. It was a lively mix of people. Some she knew, a few she did not.

Hopefully, the scandal created when she broke off her

engagement the year before had died down. Every now and then, Lauren accepted a kiss on the cheek or a handshake of greeting while continuing her conversation with Penelope. The atmosphere of acceptance was reassuring. She thought she might face more censure, even among this tight-knit group of people her cousin considered friends and family, but it appeared that was not the case at all.

"Mother is much improved. Not well enough for travel, of course, but she would not be dissuaded from my attending the festivities," Lauren replied.

Penelope, who at twenty-five was older than Lauren by two years, tilted her head just as George wrapped an arm around her waist.

"So, Lauren, you haven't decided to return to London?" he inquired with a raised brow.

Penelope looked vaguely distressed as Lauren laughed. Whipping the tartan blanket and her heavy traveling cloak from her shoulders, she handed the items off to a servant. "I've only arrived, Lord Settleton! You won't get rid of me so easily, I'm afraid."

Penelope bit her lip as the noise in the foyer abruptly ground to a halt. "Lauren, my dearest, there is something I must tell—"

It suddenly felt as though the tension in the room spiked by several degrees. An immediate shiver coursed through Lauren's body.

She knew who stood behind her. Knew *he* was the reason for the familiar tingle on the back of her neck, the sinking feeling in the pit of her stomach. For six months, he'd held claim over her, commanded her thoughts, and hijacked her breaths. When she ended things between them, his strong reaction, his anger and bewilderment, had both confused and saddened her. Many nights were wasted wondering if she'd made the right decision, just as many were spent convincing herself she had until, at last, her heart was insulated from feeling anything at all.

And now, it was happening again.

Lauren rotated, coming face to face with Theodore Samuel Hawthorne, the new Earl of Hawthorne.

Her former fiancé bowed at the waist; his eyes fixed on her as though starved for the very sight of her face. It was disturbing to realize she could not tear her gaze away from him, either.

"Hello, Lauren."

CHAPTER 2

"How ever did you talk your way into an invitation?" Lauren hissed once the library door clicked shut behind them.

Within a matter of moments, Theodore had immediately steered Lauren away from the crowd, ushering her into the first available room that offered a bit of privacy. People watched them go, whispering behind upraised hands while George and Penelope cheerfully invited everyone back to the drawing room.

Now, the earl regarded her calmly, hands clasped behind his back. His eyes roamed her body with such languid heat Lauren felt it like a physical touch.

"Perhaps you should ask your cousin what she's about. I did not pursue this, although I won't say I'm sorry we're both here. You've refused to see me, Lauren. For twelve very long months. Did you think I would forget you and move on? Because I haven't, and I won't."

"You are no longer my betrothed, Hawthorne! That sordid arrangement dissolved upon my father's death," Lauren bit out.

She remembered that day well. The day the old Earl of Hawthorne died and the discovery she'd been purchased as a bride for his son in exchange for a title came to light. She'd been heartbroken. And furious.

Theodore had known all along. When confronted, he flushed a guilty shade of red and said their marriage would take place as planned. He assured her the details of the contract didn't matter.

But it did matter, and while her father was alive, Lauren was bound to the arrangement.

It was only three months after the old earl was buried that her own father passed unexpectedly. Lord Kendall's untimely death released Lauren. While relieved to be free, she nevertheless experienced moments of deep despair. She convinced herself it was because she grieved for her father, and not because she missed Theodore.

Now she knew that was wrong. She'd missed Theodore dreadfully. Somehow, after all these months apart, the earl had grown far more handsome. Even if there was a hardness about him now, a roughness enhanced by the dark scruff shading his jaw and a wicked gleam in his eye.

Taking over his own father's bankrupt estates could not have been easy. Especially when the influx of wealth her inheritance would have provided vanished with the dissolution of their engagement.

"My father was wrong to promise me to you, and it was wrong of your father to accept that promise in exchange for money," Lauren said when she regained control of her emotions. "My mother told me you've recovered your fortunes in recent months. I am glad for it and relieved you no longer have need of my inheritance."

Theodore smiled, coming closer as Lauren instinctively retreated. She didn't realize how serious his pursuit was until her shoulder blades came in contact with one of the large windows at the room's northern end. The glass pane was icy-cold, chilling her through the layers of her clothes.

It was darker here, the sconces' light barely illuminating the shadows. Trapped by Theodore's elegantly muscled body, she was caged in place. Held hostage by a memory of melting the first time this man kissed her. How frightening it was because it seemed her soul was no longer her own. It had felt from that moment as though she belonged irrevocably to him and no one else.

How she detested the fact she had missed him.

"My lovely girl, I've no need for your inheritance." Theodore trailed a finger over Lauren's cheek. "I never held any intention of using it as a means of restoring what my irresponsible father squandered."

Theodore's icy blue eyes bore into her own grey ones, searching, probing. Lauren swallowed, wanting to look away but unable to do so. Her gaze locked on his firm mouth, which looked as kissable as ever, the lower lip full and lush and utterly sinful.

"The contract died with our fathers," Lauren whispered. "Nothing binds us together now."

"The contract still exists, although I'd never force you to honor it."

"I don't understand what you want from me, Hawthorne."

"I did not want you because of your inheritance. I agreed to marry you because I fell in love with you." Theodore leaned closer, brushing his nose along her ear, inhaling her scent. "I'm still in love with you."

"You barely know me," Lauren replied shakily. The three blissful months of their engagement before she learned of his deception also taught her a valuable lesson. Time could not reveal every nuance of a man's character.

Yes, he barely knew her, and she certainly hadn't known him.

Theodore shook his head. "Doesn't matter. The moment I laid eyes on you, I knew you were meant to be mine. You knew it, too. The first time I kissed you, you kissed me back." He tucked a stray lock of hair back into her updo and tilted her chin up with his finger. "Tell me you did not feel it too, Lauren. Tell me you did not know my heart belonged to you, and yours belonged to me."

The intensity of his gaze could not be escaped. "Your father—"

"Is dead. As is yours. What's left is between us. I want you, Lauren. I want you to be my wife. I want the opportunity to prove we should be together."

"I've no wish to be a wife." Lauren turned her head, dislodging his finger. "I want to control my own funds, make my own decisions…"

"And so you shall," Theodore agreed with cryptic smoothness. "Shielding you from fortune hunters, knowing you would become a countess, *my* countess, was your father's greatest motivation. He trusted I would take care of you for the rest of your life. Had my father not lost nearly every penny of our estates, he would never have asked Lord Kendall to consider a marriage between us. Had I not been struck by the lightning of your smile, your father would have never considered me for your husband." Theodore's head tilted, his eyes gleaming. "Tell me, Lauren. Have you not thought of me during these many months apart?"

"No."

"Liar. Your voice is trembling. You're trembling."

"I'm cold," she protested.

"That's not why you are shaking in my arms. Shall I tell you how often I think of you, Lauren? Every day. You are in my thoughts when I wake. When I retire for the evening. When I have my morning tea. When I work. When I ride my estate grounds. When I walk the gardens. Even when I sleep, I dream of you."

His head dipped toward hers until his hair tumbled into his

eyes. It was a glossy, dark chestnut hue, and so thickly luxurious it resembled mink fur. Lauren's fingers twitched with the sudden urge to brush it back from his brow. To smooth the strands into order and kiss his temples as she did so.

"Look at me, Lauren," Theodore commanded softly. "Look at me, because I have a proposition for you."

Their eyes should have clashed, hers hard with wariness, his bright with challenge. Instead, Theodore's gaze was so warm and caring, Lauren melted just a little.

"What is it?"

"For every bit of mistletoe I find you beneath, I ask that you grant me a kiss, a favor, or a truth. By Christmas, I will have changed your mind about us."

"There isn't enough mistletoe in all of England to accomplish that," she breathed.

Theodore grinned. "If I haven't convinced you by the end of Christmas Day that our marriage is precisely what you need, then I shall bother you no more. But I have overwhelming confidence in my plan."

"You are incredibly pompous."

"Without a doubt. Now, do you agree to the terms? Yes? Good. We begin."

"No. We do not begin, you ruffian," Lauren bristled, attempting to push away from the glass window and out of the cage his arms created.

She may not have agreed to his proposal, but her own words indicated compliance. There was no understanding the irresistible pull she experienced with this man. It was irrational and dangerous.

Theodore blocked her escape simply by shifting his body. Once again, he placed a finger beneath her chin, tilting until her head fell back enough to see the bow of greenery above them. Decorating the high arch of the window's frame, it filled the space between the opened draperies.

A large ball of mistletoe hung from the garland's ribbon-bedecked center. In the shadows, the plant's white berries glowed like tiny, bright stars.

"This one doesn't count, Hawthorne," Lauren choked out in alarm. Her heart accelerated, galloping twice its normal speed.

Theodore chuckled darkly, fingers sliding into her coiffure, his palm cupping her jawbone. "Oh, sweetheart. This first one counts far more than any of the others to follow. Do you even understand why you will change your mind and open your heart to me again?"

Lauren shook her head in a fractional gesture, frozen as Theodore's mouth hovered over hers. There was such an agonizing, delicious hesitancy in the gesture that a whimper of longing snagged in her throat. His hands made her dizzy. Made her remember how wonderful it felt being in his arms. How warm it made her when he smiled at her.

Forgetting he once only wanted her for her inheritance was incredibly easy. Remembering that might not have changed was even harder. Had he truly recovered his fortunes?

Theodore's winter blue eyes burned her, dark lashes shielding his true thoughts as he stroked her skin.

"It's very simple, my sweet, lonely, future wife. You need me as much as I need you. To fill the void of emptiness. To settle the restlessness in your soul. To quiet and free your desires. Give yourself to me, Lauren, and in return, I'll give you everything you never knew you wanted."

CHAPTER 3

Theodore hadn't forgotten how sweet she always smelled, like roses and vanilla. How her body curved against his own hard form as though crafted for him, her skin soft and warm as velvet.

But when his lips touched Lauren's, slanting at an angle which allowed greater access to the depths of her mouth, he realized memories paled in comparison with reality.

She tasted like ambrosia. Or the rarest brandy. Sinful and heady. Intoxicating. He wanted to drink from her until he could drink no more. Until he'd emptied her of whatever it was that fueled his hunger.

When he bit her plump, lower lip, Lauren moaned and opened her mouth further so his tongue could sweep inside. She still trembled, and Theodore moved her away from the window, wrapping his free arm around her waist and keeping her jaw cradled in the palm of his hand.

She'd been such a responsive creature before, so many months ago, leaning into his touch and eagerly accepting his kisses during their stolen moments. He was glad to see that at least had not changed.

He could not be gentle now, although he did try. In a restrained frenzy of possessiveness, he showed her how terribly he'd missed her. Showed her how desperately he still wanted her and how ironclad his resolve was.

When he finally drew back, Lauren's grey eyes were stormy and dark. Her features mirrored his own need, her skin flushed with warmth, her fingers clutching his forearm as though needing something solid to steady herself.

"I've two weeks to convince you this is where you are meant to be, Lauren. Here, in my arms. Where I can kiss you any time I desire, wherever and however I want." Theodore traced the outline of her mouth with his tongue, pushing past the seam of her lips until she parted them with a little sound of frustrated yearning.

"Hawthorne..." Lauren whispered.

"Use my name as you did once before. Don't treat this like a random social call. Do you understand me?" He ravished her mouth until she was panting. "Do you. Understand. Me?"

Her breath hitched at his unyielding tone, but she complied. "Theo."

Theodore could not deny the jolt of lust that electrified him when she said his name in a quivering sigh. His forehead dropped forward until it touched hers. "I want to devour you until I've gorged myself. Until I can't possibly take any more of you. But the truth is, I will never have my fill, Lauren. I want all of you."

Pressing one last heated kiss on her mouth, Theodore allowed her to sink back from him. His arms felt empty without her warmth.

"Now, come. Let's see you settled into your room so my conquest of your heart may begin in earnest."

∼

HOURS LATER, Theodore watched Lauren during supper. She was doing a fine job of avoiding him, and he suspected she'd engaged Penelope in making sure she was not seated anywhere near him.

He would allow that distance for now. After all, his presence here was unexpected. It probably felt as though she'd been ambushed. To be truthful, he was shocked upon arriving at Settleton the day before and learning Lauren would also be attending the house party.

The past year and a half had been brutal. His own father's death and the steps taken to rebuild the family fortune had drained him. Not to mention the guilt he'd suffered when Lauren discovered the foundation of their relationship.

He had hated hiding it from her. During their brief engagement, he debated telling Lauren the truth. He wanted to tell her how he went along with his father's wishes in the beginning for the sake of his mother. Would Lauren understand how desperately the earl wanted to ensure the wellbeing of his loved ones before his death? Even if it meant deceiving the one chosen as his bride?

Did she have any idea how frantic her own father was to protect his only child?

Lauren's musical laughter drifted from the opposite end of the table. She appeared vastly amused by something Lord Gregory Sanderson just said. She leaned toward him until the pink silk of her gown brushed his arm.

Theodore's hand clenched around the crystal goblet of wine. For a brief moment, he wanted to stalk down there, punch the other man in the mouth, and carry Lauren Georgianna Kendall out of the room. Preferably tossed over his shoulder.

"You are in danger of crushing that goblet, Hawthorne," Penelope murmured.

Theodore's gaze snapped to their hostess. She raised her own glass in a subtle toast, and he forced his fingers to relax.

"My apologies," he said with a faint smile.

"Is it too late to beg forgiveness for my part in this bizarre espionage?" Penelope's eyebrow rose slightly. "I would not blame you if you were angry with me. Lauren certainly is."

"No need. Whatever the reason, I'm glad she and I are here together. I hope to rectify matters between us… if she will allow me to do so."

"Lauren has always been stubborn." Penelope took a sip of her wine. "Even as a child, she stood her ground when we played games and someone bent the rules or cheated, and heaven help the person who thought they could make her do something she did not want to do. She has the constitution of a mule."

From the opposite side of the room, Penelope regarded Lauren for a long moment then admitted slowly, "It was both of your mothers' idea that I invite the two of you here. They are determined to see you together for your own good. I only agreed I would extend the invitation. You'll understand that I can take no further part in deceiving my cousin."

"I found it puzzling I received an invite," Theodore acknowledged.

"Did you hesitate in accepting?"

"No. Nor am I surprised my mother is involved in the plotting," he replied dryly. "She adores Lauren and fears, unless I marry her, any hope for grandchildren may be lost forever."

"You came, Hawthorne, hoping she would be here, and so she is. It is up to you now." Penelope nodded in Lauren's direction. "You have two weeks to change my cousin's mind."

"And I intend to do just that."

"How, precisely?"

Theodore flashed Penelope a wide grin. "With an ungodly amount of mistletoe." He did not mention he carried a bit of the greenery within his inner coat pocket. A good plan of action meant being prepared at all times. Especially with his surprisingly independent fiancée.

"I don't understand."

"It's a private matter between Lauren and myself. The only favor I ask of you is making sure the stuff is hung everywhere whilst we are here. You will not tell her of her mother's subterfuge."

Penelope looked unsure before nodding her agreement. "As you wish, Hawthorne."

"Thank you, Penelope. Every time Lauren turns a corner, I want a reason to kiss her, and the mistletoe will provide that until she is fully mine."

WHEN LAUREN RETIRED for the evening, Theodore made his excuses as well. He followed her from the East Drawing Room, where the others remained playing whist. Her frown of exasperation was ignored.

"Your persistence continues," she said when he fell into step alongside her.

"Just making up for lost months."

"Hmm."

"How is your mother?" Theodore asked diplomatically. "Well, I hope?"

"She is. I hope yours is the same?" Her response was polite, as he expected.

"It seems both ladies are doing better than we could have possibly imagined." Theodore sighed, thoughtfully rubbing his chin as Lauren drew up short in the grand foyer.

Gripping the newel cap of the staircase, Lauren half turned. "What do you mean?"

"It is of no matter."

"I don't believe you," Lauren said, her eyes searching his, but

Theodore merely shook his head and cupped his palm over Lauren's elbow, holding her in place.

With a crooked smile, he pointed above her head, drawing attention to greenery attached to the elaborately carved casing above the staircase. Lauren's eyes widened as he pulled her closer. "Now, you will give me a truth. Would it be so terrible, Lauren? Being my wife?"

"Theo…"

"Give me a truth." He gripped tighter, preventing her escape.

"I don't know." Lauren's voice shook a little. "Had our fathers not been involved, I would have been very happy as your wife. Before. But now, I don't know."

Theodore grit his teeth at the display of her stubborn nature. "If you cannot answer honestly, then I'll have a kiss instead."

Lauren tensed, no doubt expecting a repeat of their passionate interlude in the library, but Theodore merely raised her hand to his lips. A soft kiss was pressed to the palm of her hand.

She stared at him in shock as he released her.

"Remember my words well, Lauren. A kiss, a truth, or a favor. At the very least, I'll have one of the three."

CHAPTER 4

*L*auren rolled over, propping her arm under a pillow, and watched Anne bustle about the room. It was barely nine o'clock in the morning. Pity she could not sleep any later, especially after tossing and turning all night.

"The hot chocolate is ready, milady," the maid said. "Will you want it by the fire, or shall I bring it to you in bed?"

"In bed," Lauren replied, sitting up. "It's too cold to get up just yet."

"That it is," Anne agreed with a laugh. She handed a delicate cup to Lauren, then continued readying the bath set up before the fire.

By the time Lauren finished her hot chocolate, the last bit of steaming water was added to the slipper tub. With a reluctant sigh, she threw back the coverlet and slid from the bed, her toes curling upon contact with the cold floor.

Anne took her nightrail, placing it neatly over a chair before helping her into the tub. Sinking into the steamy water with a sigh, Lauren grinned at her maid.

"I might stay here all day."

"Not once that water begins to chill, milady. You'll jump out fast as a cat when that happens. I'll be back in a bit to help you dress and arrange your hair, but I'm off to check on Mr. Ollie. He's still feeling poorly after riding on top of that coach, the stubborn thing."

"Take your time, Anne. If Ollie is in need of anything, please let the housekeeper know. A few days of rest would certainly benefit him, and you as well." Lauren tilted her head. "In fact, other than helping me with gowns that button up the back, I see no reason for you to attend me with such diligence."

"Oh, milady. Arrange your own hair? Dress yourself, too? What sort of lady's maid would I be if I allowed that?"

"The sort who deserves a day or two for herself. Truly, Anne, it will please me to give you that. Plus, you can look in on Ollie. I'm certain he will want you near."

Anne appeared unconvinced but hopeful. "I don't know, milady. Are you sure?"

Lauren smiled. "Of course. Go on now. Take your time and come back when you are ready."

"Oh, Lady Lauren! You are too good to me." A huge grin broke across Anne's face. "Thank you."

Anne exited in a flurry of skirts while Lauren chuckled and relaxed back against the edge of the tub.

In the silence of the room, with only the crackling of the fire to disturb the calm, Lauren contemplated the true motives behind her actions. Yes, she was being kind to her servants, but she also did not want any witnesses to whatever that devil, Lord Hawthorne, had planned.

The nerve of the man. Using something as commonplace as a bit of weed to prove her desire for him. It wasn't fair he could command her responses so easily. She couldn't forget he meant to trick her into marriage a second time.

And yet, how could she ignore the way her body ignited when Theo touched her?

Staring into the flames of the fire, Lauren was so embroiled in her thoughts that the click of the door did not register.

The trailing of a forefinger down the nape of her neck, exposed by her upswept hair, alerted her that she wasn't alone.

With a startled gasp, Lauren sank further into the tub. Water sloshed over the sides when she instinctively crossed her arms over bare breasts.

"Good morning, my sweet," Theodore drawled, his hand curling into a light grip on her neck. "Did you sleep you well? I didn't. Too many thoughts of you running through my mind, unfortunately."

"Have you taken complete leave of your senses?" Lauren choked out. "Have you no regard for the scandal this could cause?" She thought her heart would pound out of her chest from the fright he just gave her. Thank goodness Anne added some rose oil to the bathwater. It clouded the water just enough that Lauren could retain a bit of her modesty.

Theodore stood beside the tub, his fingers caressing her nape as he stared down at her. His full lips quirked upward with a slight twist.

"No one else is about this early in the morning, and Anne told me she had no intention of returning for a while. I have the feeling she was encouraging me to check in on you."

He was dressed for riding, although Lauren could not imagine anyone willing to venture out in such freezing temperatures. Wearing a pair of dark breeches, a white shirt, and a knee-high Hessians, he also carried a wool riding coat in the crook of his arm. She watched as he carelessly tossed it onto the same chair as her nightrail.

Her heart rate ratcheted with something suspiciously akin to desire when he teased her earlobe, the blunt ends of his fingernails grazing her flesh. "Please, Theo. You shouldn't be here…"

"When we are wed, this will become part of our morning routine. I will play lady's maid for you. I will gladly wash your hair, pour the oils in your bath. Cleanse your body, from your head to the tips of your toes. And everything in between."

While he spoke, his fingers traveled from her earlobe to the slope of her shoulder, then down along the delicate line of her collarbone. Lauren sucked in a breath, sinking further into the water, but that did not deter him.

Pulling a sprig of mistletoe from a small pocket of his breeches, he dangled it over her forehead, then tucked it away when she frowned up at him. This mistletoe business was becoming quite ridiculous. Did he intend on carrying the blasted plant with him everywhere he went? Did he mean to back her into a corner at every turn with it?

Chuckling, Theodore moved closer and gripped her chin with his free hand. With gentle pressure, he forced her gaze to meet his. His blue eyes were so bright with promise that Lauren felt her heart squeeze in response even through her frustrated anger.

"I can show you more pleasure than you could ever imagine, my love, by simply touching you," he murmured, fingers dancing between the exposed border of flesh and the silky skin beneath the water's edge. "But I will not take from you what you are unwilling to give. Tell me to leave and I will go."

The demand was on the very tip of her tongue, but the words died a quick death. Lauren could only swallow and gaze up at him, wondering what pleasures he spoke of. What delights could be experienced with a mere brush of his fingers?

The longer she remained mute, the more it appeared she wished him to stay.

"Lauren?" Theodore's hand tightened on her chin, his thumb rising to graze her lower lip as though testing its softness.

Lauren had no idea what possessed her, she really didn't, but her lips parted slightly as she stared into the wintery indigo depths of Theodore's eyes. Her tongue darted out, swiping at his thumb in quick exploration before she let him push it further into the depths of her mouth.

Something very wicked and primal and unbearably wild roared to life inside her when she observed his hunger.

Yes, he will consume me, drown me in lust and want. I'm foolish enough to believe I can withstand the onslaught and not long for more.

Theodore's eyes burned as he moved his thumb deeper until her tongue curled around it, and her mouth closed over it with an innocent understanding of what he wanted. So intent was Lauren on watching his eyes as they ignited into twin flames that she truly did not pay heed to his other hand until suddenly it was below the waterline. Touching her breasts. Smoothing the globes alternately with his palm, measuring and caressing until Lauren's back arched the slightest bit, and her breasts broke the water's surface.

A muscle ticked in Theodore's clenched jaw, but his hand remained steady as he stroked her.

"A favor I will take this time."

His words were a growled rumble that oddly enough vibrated inside her chest as if he'd cut her open and deposited them there.

Then his fingers plucked one taut, dusky rose nipple, quickly followed by the same treatment of the other, and Lauren moaned softly. Almost convulsively, she swallowed around his thumb, unable to stop herself from doing so again and again as he softly pinched and tweaked the pebbled, sensitive peaks of her breasts.

Pressure was building within her, sparking the nerves hidden behind the soft folds at the apex of her thighs. It was unbearable. She wanted him to touch her there. To thrust his fingers deep inside her and extinguish the raging fire.

It was torture. It was pleasure. It was everything she never realized she needed. Now she wanted it all, and in the midst of the whirlwind, she hated Theodore Hawthorne for awakening this hunger.

"You are so beautiful, Lauren." Theodore's voice was a gravelly mix of desire and awe. "I cannot wait for the day you are truly mine. How foolish you've been, keeping yourself from me."

Lauren froze as if drenched by a bucket of cold water. Giving his thumb a sharp, little nip, she shoved him away at the same time.

Jerking away with a low growl, Theodore examined the tiny wound then sucked off the drop of blood. For a heartbeat, his eyes narrowed while he studied Lauren's face, almost as if he couldn't believe she'd snapped at him.

"The day I am yours?" Lauren spat. "I still haven't forgiven you for lying to me, so I can't say for certain I'll ever be yours. You've had your fun this morning, Hawthorne, with your silly mistletoe. Now, get out of my room before I scream this house down around your ears."

The threat did not seem to faze him in the least. With a low bow, he turned and scooped up his coat.

"I'll go, Lauren." The smile he gave her was unnerving, but far more unsettling was the moment he leaned forward and tipped her chin up so he could stare into her eyes. "We shall finish this later."

CHAPTER 5

*E*ach time Theodore closed his eyes, he saw Lauren's breasts. Perfect. Round. Slightly bigger than the palm of his hand and tipped with the most delectable rose-hued nipples.

Given the chance, he would have played with her all day. Would have bent his head and tasted those lovely peaks after teasing them to stand at stiff attention. Would have slid his hand down her flat, silken stomach until he speared the damp curls between her thighs. He would have swallowed her whimpers of pleasure as he penetrated her tight passage with his fingers and stroked her to completion.

Theodore rubbed a hand over his face, mentally scrubbing away the images from his brain.

Lauren was proving quite resistant to his attempts thus far, although he sensed her underlying weakness. He'd awoken a tiny flame of desire deep within her. Fanning those flames higher would require ruthless dedication. He would not relent until she realized how much he truly loved her and how he regretted his role in what their fathers had done.

While waiting for Lauren's appearance downstairs,

Theodore took notice of the abundance of mistletoe hung around the mansion. It adorned nearly every passageway, doorway, and window that he could see. Penelope even took the opportunity of having it dangled from the chandeliers.

There were not many places Lauren would be safe, and that pleased him greatly.

"Why are you not gone?" Lauren asked behind him, sounding quite vexed.

Pivoting toward her, his grin widened at the sight of her standing in the entrance to the dining room.

He bit back a laugh when she glanced heavenward and then rushed forth so she wasn't caught beneath the kissing bough again.

"Gone?" Theodore's brow raised, taking in the butter-hued morning dress she wore. It complimented her rich brown hair and its honey-streaked highlights perfectly. He wondered how long her hair was. He'd never seen it down—it was always in some kind of bun or elaborate updo.

Today, it was piled into a shining mass high on her head, the straight length wrapped around itself in a braided coronet. Wispy tendrils brushed her ears, softening the effect. It looked lovely on her, reminding him again how tender the exposed nape of her neck was.

"Yes. Gone. I thought you were riding this morning?"

Theodore seated himself at the table, watching one of the servants pour coffee for him. He'd taken a liking to the stuff. Thank God Penelope and George served it as occasionally he desired something a bit stronger than an insipid cup of tea.

"I am. Care to join me?" he offered politely.

Lauren bit her lip before shaking her head. "It's far too cold for riding. Besides, Penelope asked that the ladies prepare sweetmeat and almond papers today for decorating the tree."

"Sounds incredibly boring."

Theodore thought she might reprimand him, but after a

moment, she sighed in agreement. "It does. But regardless, it's still too cold for riding."

He couldn't believe she was actively, albeit not enthusiastically, subtly seeking his company.

"We could go ice skating instead." Sipping his coffee, Theodore watched over the cup's rim as she slid into the chair beside his.

"Still rather cold..." Lauren frowned, picking up a fork and testing the sharpness of the tines.

"We could have a fire near the water's edge. A few blankets..." He poured her a cup of tea, dismissing a hovering servant with a wave of his hand. "Settleton says the pond is frozen solid."

Lauren accepted the cup pushed toward her, dropping two sugar cubes into the steaming liquid. She stirred the tea with a tiny silver spoon while considering him beneath a fringe of dark lashes, her eyes twin pools of cloudy grey.

"I've never ice skated before."

"I'll show you how it's done," Theodore immediately offered.

The look she gave him was frankly suspicious, and Theodore could not help but laugh. But before he could voice any assurances that he held no ulterior motives, George and Lord Sanderson bustled into the room.

Theodore's eyes narrowed to see Sanderson's face light up when he realized Lauren was seated at the table. He wanted to stand and block the man's path when he strode toward her.

With great effort, Theodore remained seated.

"Lady Lauren, how wonderful to discover you are an early riser like myself!" Sanderson lifted her hand, pressed a kiss to it, then took the chair on her opposite side while Theodore grit his teeth. George plopped down at the head of the table, a curious expression crossing his handsome face.

"A habit developed during my time away from society,"

Lauren murmured, sipping her tea again. "Mornings have become my favorite time of the day."

Theodore relaxed in his chair with a lazy grin. "Mornings often start with the best of surprises."

Lauren's eyes shot to his, and his lazy grin left no doubt he referred to the intrusion of her bedchamber earlier. Her mouth tightened, her cheeks turning a delicious shade of pink at the reminder.

"What are your plans for the day, Lady Lauren?" Sanderson inquired, touching her elbow.

"I'm not sure—" she began when Theodore interrupted, his voice coolly aloof.

"We are going ice skating."

Sanderson blinked at his tone, and George's brow rose slightly before Theodore's apparent rival recovered.

"Ice skating? I say, that sounds like just the thing. What do you think, Settleton? We could all make an afternoon of it as I'm sure there are others who would enjoy the bracing winter air and an opportunity to exhibit their skills." Sanderson exclaimed in excitement, "Yes, it's a wonderful idea."

If it's so bloody wonderful, why does the idea of others around us annoy me? Theodore brooded as George shot him a covert glance before granting his approval of the plan.

Before Theodore knew what was happening, the quiet interlude with Lauren was completely taken over. While this turn of events irritated him beyond belief, Lauren seemed quite pleased.

The twinkle in her eyes was taken as a challenge he could not and would not ignore.

Under the clatter of breakfast dishes being set up by the servants, Theodore whispered in Lauren's ear, "Be warned, sweetheart. The woods around that pond are full of mistletoe. You couldn't drag me away with a team of horses now."

CHAPTER 6

*L*auren huddled closer to the circle of stones making up a rather large firepit. Several iron benches provided seating, and if one desired a mug of hot apple cider to warm their insides, a large vat of the beverage was kept warm in the coals.

Curling her gloved hands around the tin cup, Lauren smiled as she watched Penelope and George glide arm and arm. Her lovely cousin gazed at the viscount in obvious adoration, her laughter echoing across the open space with that of the other guests.

A tiny frisson of envy struck Lauren without warning. The unwelcome emotion was startling, but most confusing was why on earth her gaze unerringly sought out the Earl of Hawthorne.

He'd reluctantly left her behind after she refused his command to join him on the pond's frozen surface. Now, he slid effortlessly over the ice, his forearm held tight by a simpering chit.

A second cousin to George, Lady Melanie Overton was blonde, willowy, and quite the flirt. Lauren had met her several times at various social functions. While cordial to one another, their interactions never progressed any further than that, and Penelope once confessed to Lauren her dislike for the girl.

Now, Lauren watched helplessly as Melanie stumbled and Theodore easily steadied her with an arm slipped around her waist. Pulling her tighter against his body, he said something that made the lady laugh. Then she turned slightly until it almost appeared as though they danced the waltz on steel blades.

Dropping her gaze, Lauren swallowed past the lump in her throat. Even with the warmth of the vessel in her hands and the heat of the flames from the firepit, she shivered.

"Shall I procure a blanket, Lady Lauren?" Lord Sanderson plopped down on the bench with an easygoing smile. Slipping the ice-skates from his feet, he set them aside.

"That would be very kind." A few moments later, a thick, red woolen blanket lay draped about her shoulders.

"There. That should do the trick until you decide to venture onto the ice. The exertion warms the blood very quickly, I find."

"I believe I shall return to the house once I've finished my cider." Lauren gave him an apologetic smile, fighting the urge to stare in the direction of the pond when a peal of laughter rang out.

It sounded suspiciously like Lady Melanie Overton.

"Oh, that won't do at all! You've not even taken a turn around the pond. Come, I'll help you. You shan't fall as long as you hold on to me," Sanderson urged. "I'll find you a pair of skates, and you'll see it's grand fun."

Lauren said nothing. Taking another sip of cider, she dared a peek toward the pond and wished she hadn't.

Coming toward them, Theodore and Melanie trudged through a thin layer of snow. Melanie was laughing with delight, cheeks pink with exertion while the earl oddly enough seemed to be biting the inside of his cheek. His eyes were pools of icy blue when they slid over Lauren and Sanderson sitting so cozily together.

Finding an empty bench across from them, the pair sat down, Theodore's long legs stretching almost obscenely in Lauren's direction. She nearly winced as Melanie snuggled closer as if warming herself simply by hugging his arm.

"It's dreadfully cold once you stop moving, isn't it?" Melanie exclaimed, her teeth biting her bottom lip in a pretty gesture as she gazed up at Theodore.

"I was explaining to Lady Lauren, if she only took a turn, she would warm up nicely," Sanderson offered. "I'm afraid she doesn't believe me, however. Perhaps you can convince her, Lady Melanie. After all, you appear quite flushed."

Melanie's eyelashes fluttered as she acknowledged Lord Sanderson, and Lauren experienced the overwhelming urge to rip the feathery things out by their roots.

"Ice-skating may not be completely at fault," she simpered, giving Theodore another besotted look before gracefully removing the skates from her dainty feet. "Lord Hawthorne believes I'm in danger of twisting an ankle, so we agreed I should rest for a moment." By her tone, she had every expectation Theodore would rest along with her.

"This is a perfect opportunity!" Sanderson crowed, retrieving Melanie's skates before Lauren could form a protest. Kneeling in front of her with the things in hand, he reached beneath her skirts.

With a low growl, Theodore rose to his feet. In two steps, he was towering over the other man.

"What the devil do you think you are doing, Sanderson? Get your blasted hands off of her."

With a ruthless shove, Theodore knocked Sanderson away from Lauren and just as quickly took his place, unmindful of the damage the snow might do to his trousers. "If anyone will be touching these lovely ankles, it shall be myself alone," he muttered beneath his breath.

"I say, Hawthorne, I am perfectly capable of helping Lady Lauren," Sanderson stuttered in outraged surprise.

Theodore shot him a savage glare. "No."

Just a single word. That was all. Nothing more, but it was enough for Sanderson to shrink back as though punched. Scrambling up, he took a seat beside Melanie, who looked infuriated to see her skates being placed on Lauren's feet.

Lauren's pulse raced as Theodore's fingers trailed over the fine bones of her ankles while the straps of the skates were tightened. She was too stunned to voice an objection as he took her mug of cider, placed it aside, and pulled her upright.

When she wobbled like a newborn foal on spindly legs, his arm snaked around her waist as she'd seen him do with Melanie.

"It is a short distance to the pond, Lauren," Theodore said in a low voice, and while she'd been shivering just moments before, she was definitely warm now with the heat of his body pressed against hers. "Lean against my shoulder if you need to."

He was daring her to defy him, although, in her current mood, she wasn't sure she could manage it. With a stubborn tilt of her chin, she braved a few tentative steps, his muscled arms acting as a brace. A quick glance at Melanie revealed the lady watching them with narrowed eyes, a glint of jealousy evident in their depths.

In a matter of seconds, Theodore had pulled her onto the pond, and Lauren experienced a stab of fear when her feet quickly slid independently of her wishes. She clutched at him.

"Theodore!" Her terrified squeak drew a reassuring grin from him. Other skaters wisely gave them a wide berth, and Theodore kept along the edges of the pond.

"Hold on to me, sweetheart." He steadied her once more, his

body something akin to a sturdy oak. "Now, the most important rule of ice skating is you must never look at your feet."

"What?" Lauren frowned. "That is the silliest thing I've ever heard." Immediately, she glanced down and suffered a quick wobble that made Theodore tighten his hold even more.

Placing a forefinger beneath her chin, he lifted it until their gazes locked. "See? Eyes up. In fact, keep them on me, Lauren."

"I don't want to fall," she whispered, staring at him while fighting the urge to look at their feet. Were they actually moving, and were they still discussing ice skating? "It will hurt, and I'm frightened."

"I know." Theodore was calm, maneuvering her in a way that should have been disturbing but somehow put her at ease. She relaxed the tiniest bit against his side as he murmured, "But if you fall, I fall as well. All right?"

Lauren slowly nodded, keeping her eyes on him.

"Now, do you trust me?" he asked, and when she hesitated, he gave her that smile that never failed to make her head fuzzy. The one that made his sky-blue eyes sparkle like diamonds and was both wicked and mischievous. When he smiled at her like that, she thought she might agree with just about anything he asked of her. "Do you trust me, Lauren?" he prodded.

"Yes."

There was no time to overthink her surrender. Withdrawing his arm from her waist, he rotated so they faced one another and took both her hands within his own gloved ones. Using strong pushes of his thighs, Theodore moved backward in a move oddly similar to dancing.

"Eyes on me. Hold on to my hands. I'll pull you… Now, move your feet a little, side to side. Tiny, alternating movements. There. Just like that, sweetheart. You are doing amazing. You're nearly skating by yourself."

Concentrating on Theodore's features made it easy to forget her fear of falling. Basking in the warmth of his smile made her wish he would always look at her like this. The cold air stung her cheeks, and Lauren wondered if, without the skates, perhaps he might have pulled her closer to his body, held her so she could feel his breath on her neck. Maybe even brush his lips against her ear. Or press his mouth upon hers.

I want him to kiss me. But unless he carried that blasted mistletoe in his pocket, there was no good reason he would.

Longing for something so dangerous buckled Lauren's knees.

Her hands ripped free from Theodore's. Landing with a thump, the pain at first knocked the breath from her lungs. Thrown off balance, Theodore fell to the ice as well.

A helpless giggle tumbled from Lauren at the comical sight of the fiercely elegant and habitually proper earl sprawled on his bum beside her. That quickly morphed into a chuckle, and before she knew it, she was laughing so hard she couldn't breathe.

Theodore stared at her for a long moment, concern for her safety obvious in the way his eyes traveled over her. Then, his lips twitched with the hint of a grin. Moving closer, his hand slid up to cup her jaw, the leather of his glove surprisingly warm as though his skin radiated heat beneath the material. Lauren fought the urge to nestle into his touch even while she laughed.

Finally, a reluctant chuckle broke free from Theodore, his eyes roaming over her curved mouth until she licked her lips self-consciously. When he spoke, the words were a husky rasp of familiarity and restrained desire.

"God, how I've missed your laughter. Hearing it now makes up for my bruised posterior."

"Are you truly injured, or is it only your ego that has suffered?" she teased, almost forgetting they sat on a frozen pond in a jumble of skirts and legs and sharp, steel skates while people glided past, throwing them curious stares. It was quite scandalous they'd not made a single effort to rise from the ice. "I told you I was afraid of falling."

"And I told you I'd go down as well."

Suddenly sober, Theodore eased forward until their noses nearly touched, until Lauren thought he might actually kiss her.

"Let me in, Lauren, and you'll never fall alone."

CHAPTER 7

They lagged behind the others during the walk back to the manor.

Lauren was oddly quiet, but Theodore could not stop thinking how completely her laughter entranced him. How it left him more determined than ever to capture and claim her for his own.

When he stopped short on the pathway, she did not protest but merely regarded him with such calm Theodore wanted to shake her.

"Leave your door unlocked tonight, Lauren."

"Why would I do that?"

"Why would you not? We've matters between us unsettled from this morning. Remember?" Theodore said in a low voice.

Lauren appeared disconcerted for a moment, then her mouth tightened. "I will remind you again; you are not my betrothed."

"Damn it all, Lauren." His words came out in a growl. Pulling her off the path so no one could witness his actions, he backed her against an English yew tree, his hands tight on her shoulders. "Why do you fight what is between us? Jesus Christ,

I'm willing to give you anything your heart desires just to have you."

Lauren shoved him, although the effort proved ineffective. Her chin jerked up, bringing Theodore's attention to a bit of wild mistletoe tangled in the branches above their heads. "Give me a truth, Theo. Why did you not tell me what was done before I confronted you with it? Why didn't *you* tell me I'd been bought for my inheritance?"

"Do you have any idea how difficult it was for me to take care of my estates, to provide for my mother and all those dependent upon me once you voided our engagement contract? Do you?" Theodore countered angrily. "And to keep it all secret on top of that?

Lauren remained stubbornly silent until he rubbed her bottom lip with the pad of his gloved thumb. She let out a tiny gasp as he gruffly spoke. "I would not have used your inheritance; however, the idea it *was* available carried tremendous weight with my father's creditors."

Tears built in her eyes until they shone like diamonds in the weak winter sunshine. "I was so happy when you asked me to marry you. I truly thought you loved me."

"I did," Theodore swore. "Goddamnit, I still do."

"You used me. Perhaps not intentionally, but you did, and you would have continued using me had I not severed our relationship. It's just as awful as my father using your family to gain his daughter a title." Lauren pushed him away when his hands abruptly dropped to his sides. Ducking past him, she shook out her skirts and gave him what could only be considered a pitying look. "That is *our* truth, Theodore."

THAT IS OUR TRUTH, Theodore.

Lauren's words needled Theodore. Through the rest of that

afternoon, into the evening, through the night and into the next day, as she evaded his company and surrounded herself with the few single men her cousin invited to the house party, those words taunted and prodded him.

So, she believed she'd been used for his own gain. He squirmed uncomfortably, knowing she suffered under that disillusion. His motives for remaining silent on the terms of their engagement were oddly enough to spare Lauren both pain and embarrassment. No one needed to know his family bought themselves a rich bride, and inheritance or no, once he met Lauren, he was determined to have her, no matter what.

As his valet tied his cravat, preparing him for the evening meal, Theodore remembered the night he asked Lauren for her hand in marriage.

It was at the Pettiman Ball. They'd stepped onto the terrace for a bit of fresh air after a rousing Scottish reel. Slipping his arms around Lauren's tiny waist, he kissed her until she was breathless. Then, with the moonlight reflecting in her eyes, he told her he loved her and asked her to be his wife.

An instant "Yes!" and arms thrown around his neck was Lauren's immediate response. Their engagement was announced that very evening, just before the last waltz. It was incredibly romantic, the talk of the society pages for weeks, and completely staged by their fathers for maximum effect.

He and Lauren enjoyed a whirlwind courtship of stolen kisses and increasingly passionate embraces before his father finally succumbed to wasting disease. Theodore was saddened but not broken. Now, there was a chance to repair things his own way.

The promise of Lauren's inheritance eased the way. Creditors ready to call for his head backed off, willing to give Theodore a chance to work on alternative measures when it came to repaying the debts.

But that only lasted until Lauren's own father died unexpectedly three months later. When she broke off their engagement, all hell broke loose.

The overwhelming mountain of liabilities, the pressure in caring for his mother, the estates, the tenants, had Theodore solving issues the only way he knew how. By using his own wits and calling in favors from everyone who owed him. Through cunning and incredible luck, he rebuilt his family's fortune until it was richer than before his father lost it all.

But Lauren didn't know about that. She only knew he agreed to marry her for her money. No matter how often he claimed otherwise, she wouldn't believe him until he proved her wrong.

Theodore sighed, waving the valet away with an impatient gesture.

He would work harder at convincing Lauren. Think of some way of demonstrating his devotion and love for her.

But what could he do when she already had everything she needed?

$$\sim$$

FOLLOWING SUPPER, Penelope and George gathered all the guests in the main salon.

"Gentlemen, we have games of chance for your pleasure," George announced. "Ladies, there is whist if you are so inclined. Or you may watch from the sidelines."

Theodore made his way to Lauren's side. She was ravishing in a deep, emerald green gown, beaded ebony jets decorating the low-cut bodice. Again, her hair was swept up into a chignon, with wispy ends fluttering around her ears and leaving her nape enticingly exposed. Black satin, elbow-length gloves completed her ensemble.

"Will you play?" he asked, devouring her in the flattering light cast by the chandeliers overhead.

"Perhaps." Lauren's attention remained on her cousin as

Penelope floated from table to table, ensuring the games were ready for play. The excitement level rose by several degrees, conversations growing louder and more boisterous as wine and spirits began flowing. "Wouldn't you prefer a game of baccarat?"

"I prefer a turn of cards, so my fortunes are in my own hands rather than the capricious spin of a wheel."

Her gaze cut to him, stormy rainclouds that never failed to remind Theodore of drowning. "Your father was fond of baccarat. Or so I heard."

It was the first time Lauren had broached the root cause of his family's financial ruin. Theodore's teeth clenched with embarrassment. He'd known one day this particular subject would raise its head.

Why he had needed an heiress.

"That's true. My father gambled his holdings, my future, everything my mother brought to the marriage. He wasted it all, then stood amongst the ruins and begged that I marry well enough to overcome his losses."

It nearly killed him to see Lauren's bottom lip tremble with his statement. Before he could soothe her, a servant stepped up, handing them two glasses of wine.

Lauren took the glass with a murmured 'thank you' while Theodore wanted to dash his to the floor, gather the woman before him into his arms, and kiss her until she forgot her anger with him. Forgot his arrogance when she confronted him so many months ago. Forgot his culpability in concealing their fathers' plan. Most of all, he wanted her to forget he'd not trusted her to still love him once she learned the truth.

Theodore stared at her, struck by all the things he suddenly wished to say. But as if entangled in a web, the words jammed in his throat, refusing to advance.

He took Lauren's elbow in his hand.

"Lauren..."

"Ah-ah," she scolded under her breath, pulling free of his

grasp. "There's no mistletoe where I'm standing. Which is surprising because this entire house is dripping in the stuff."

"Would you consider having a conversation where we would have more privacy?"

Lauren glanced in the direction Theodore indicated, a window alcove where a single kissing ball hung, and gave him a fierce scowl. "Are you serious?"

"We must talk…"

"Must we?" Her words were sweet enough, but her eyes flashed at him.

"Yes. We must." Before he could elaborate, Lady Melanie sidled up to him.

"Lord Hawthorne, there you are. Would you partner me in a game of whist? I'm quite good at it. There is no fear we shall lose."

Cutting the lady a brief glance, Theodore bit out, "My apologies, my lady. I'm otherwise occupied."

Melanie pouted, which may have had the desired effect on another man. It only left Theodore feeling irritated, especially when her attention allowed Lauren to edge away. And blast it all, Sanderson was waiting nearby, ready to pounce on Lauren the moment Theodore's back was turned. Lords Jenkins and Harland stood alongside him, their eyes trained on the woman he intended on marrying.

Theodore's blood grew hotter as it traveled the path of his veins. His hands clenched into fists. He wanted to attack all the scoundrels and beat them to a pulp for even daring to look at Lauren. They were practically stripping her clothes from her body; they stared so intently. The scowl he sent them was so fierce the three men hastily averted their eyes, turned their bodies in the opposite direction of Lauren, and promptly stumbled into each other like bumbling fools.

"Oh, please, Lord Hawthorne! You simply must help me…" Melanie pleaded, mouth pursed into a pout.

"You cannot mean to make a lady beg your mercy, Hawthorne," Lauren cut in, eyes sparkling with mischief. "That would be most cruel."

Theodore choked back a response. He had every intention of making Lauren beg for his mercy. Preferably in the privacy of her room. Away from anyone who might think to rescue her.

Melanie latched onto his arm. Without making a scene, Theodore knew he could not dislodge the woman.

"Oh, Penelope has need of me," Lauren said, her gaze landing somewhere beyond Theodore and Melanie. "I do wish you luck at whist."

Before Theodore could stop her, she glided away.

CHAPTER 8

*L*auren watched until she could take no more.

Jealousy twisted her insides as Melanie hung on Theodore's every word, as well as his arm. At one point, she even draped herself on his shoulder, laughing.

"You must say one thing for her." Penelope pressed a second glass of wine into Lauren's hand with a chuckle. "She is persistent."

"And beautiful." Lauren sighed.

"If it is any consolation, Hawthorne has avoided her. He's not provided escort to any lady as far as I am aware. It's been a source of gossip. Especially considering you broke off your engagement and he was technically free to pursue another."

"I would not care if he did pursue another." Lauren shifted her feet. She fought the urge to glance at the couple again when Melanie's trill of laughter drifted over the saloon. It was just a touch louder than the three-piece stringed quartet hired from the village. "Our association is over."

Penelope tilted her blonde head, regarding Lauren with a perceptive eye. "Is it, my dear? It does not appear so. I think you are not quite at ease with another woman's interest in your former fiancé." Theodore's form was subjected to a calculating assessment. "One cannot fault the ladies for it, however. He is a fine specimen of a man, and with his title and fortune, well, it's easy to see why they adore him so." Adjusting a few baubles on the Christmas tree, Penelope smiled. "I'm glad you are not still cross with me, cousin."

"The reasons for my anger were selfish." Lauren desperately ignored the leap in her pulse at the reminder of Theodore's darkly dangerous good looks. How many times had she nearly drowned in his winter blue eyes the afternoon before? Far more than she wished to count. "After all, it is not my place to dictate your guest list. I would know, however, whether the earl was invited before or after I accepted your invitation."

Penelope sipped her wine before answering, and Lauren could not help but think if that was her cousin's way of gaining more time to form a response.

"They were sent at the same time. Honestly, I doubted Hawthorne would accept, although I suppose he hoped you would attend."

"Perhaps he desired other company." Noticing Melanie's hand casually draped along the top of Theodore's thigh, danger-ously close to his lap, Lauren winced. Was it her imagination, or did his muscles jump beneath the fine wool of his trousers?

"You can't believe that's true. The man has hunted you from the moment you arrived. I've no idea what scandal led to the demise of your engagement, but do not doubt he is devoted to having you for his wife, Lauren."

"He betrayed me," Lauren whispered absently, watching Theodore murmur into Melanie's ear. Curiously, the lady scowled, removing her hand from his leg with amazing speed.

"With another woman? I don't believe that at all. From the moment you met, it was plain you were meant for one another," Penelope scoffed.

"I—I really don't want to talk about this, Penelope." Lauren drew herself up straighter while cringing at the thought of Theodore lavishing attention on anyone else. "I fear I'm not proving very festive. Perhaps the journey here is finally catching up to me." *Or perhaps my efforts in eluding Theodore have exhausted me.*

Penelope slipped an arm around Lauren. "Dear cousin, I've no wish to pry, but might I offer a bit of advice? From a married woman's perspective, if you will have it." At Lauren's reluctant nod, the viscountess prodded, "If a man is striving to prove you have his attention, or apologizing when he hasn't shown the inclination of doing so before, please consider its worth."

"What are you saying, precisely?" Lauren breathed.

"Give Hawthorne a chance, my dear. He may surprise you with his sincerity."

Lauren pondered her cousin's advice as the atmosphere in the salon grew increasingly jovial. Sitting in on a few hands of vingt-et-un, she lost abysmally because her mind was not on the game. Then she stood by, watching as several brave souls played Snapdragon until all the raisins in the bowl of flaming brandy were gone.

Rather aimlessly, she wandered about the large, boisterous room, acutely aware of the instant Theodore broke free of the whist game.

From a deceptively casual stance by the large fireplace, his back against the wall and a glass of brandy in one hand, Theodore's dark gaze followed Lauren. Even though engaged in conversation with other lords over recent parliamentary matters, his attention sent a shiver up her spine even while he kept his distance.

A small blessing, Lauren conceded. The earl's predatory nature was enough that men such as Lord Sanderson dared not venture close at all for the moment. She was unsure how long that might last.

In the midst of the evening's activities and chatter, a small group of servants wheeled in two tea carts. Lined up in neat little rows were footed porcelain bowls filled with fresh snow and a pitcher containing a syrupy mixture of lemon juice and sugar.

"Oh!" One lady clapped her hands. "We're having ices just like at Gunter's!"

This was met with surprised exclamations of delight. Those not seated at the gaming tables gathered around the tea carts, eagerly accepting servings of the treat. Lauren was momentarily distracted by someone's enthusiastic shout of triumph over a favorable turn of cards and did not notice Theodore sliding into the open space by her side.

She was immediately wary but refused to flee.

He handed her a bowl. "I remember how fond you are of desserts like this."

"Thank you," Lauren muttered, swallowing a deep breath when their fingers brushed.

Theodore's full lips quirked with a smile, leaving no doubt he was aware of her reaction.

Lifting her spoon, Lauren took a dainty nibble of the ice as if she hadn't just come close to losing her composure. "It's very good. Don't you care for some, my lord?"

She froze in the process of taking another bite once she realized his eyes were riveted on her mouth.

"Will you feed it to me yourself, Lauren?" A hint of a smile twitched at his lips.

She blinked, and he was suddenly even closer.

"Of course not," she stammered. "What a preposterous suggestion—"

"Then allow me the pleasure to do so for you..." Theodore's voice lowered an octave, and it seemed as though they were the only two occupants in the room. Everything else, the noise, the laughter, the gaiety, all faded away. The earl's eyes, so deep and mesmerizing, held hers. Lauren did not realize she was trapped like a rabbit in a snare until his finger gently traced the bare skin above her gloves.

She didn't move away. No, to the contrary, she held still and held her breath, waiting for Theodore to do something more. Something… scandalous. Wicked. Even in a crowded room, there was no doubt the man would do as he pleased.

"You know you cannot do that, Theo. Besides, I'm not a child to be spoon-fed."

"Eventually, you will admit I can do what I like with you, Lauren. I am finding the waiting for your acceptance of that fact to be tedious."

"What *would* you do with me?" Lauren asked, her mouth curving with a little smile.

"Ah, now you tease me."

Lauren blushed. "I'm not. I only wonder…"

"Come with me, Lauren."

"Why?" she whispered.

"Because I want you to." Theodore's head tilted as he watched her reaction to his demand. No one could see, but his finger inched from the back of her elbow to the side of her breast. Lauren trembled while he stroked the curve there. Even through the satin of her dress, the heat of his fingertips melted and burned her skin. "Because it's time I show you exactly what I will do with you. You will goddamn love it; I promise you that," he said in a deceptively calm voice. "Go wait for me in the west hall."

When he removed the bowl of lemon ice from her hand, Lauren could not find an objection within her indignation at being ordered so cavalierly. Her breathing had gone shallow, her cheeks flushed with warmth, and a terrible, frightening excitement raced along the network of her veins. This was dangerous. Dangerous and yet unavoidable.

"I won't ask again," he hissed in her ear, his lips brushing the fragile skin. "Go."

Lauren did as commanded. Even though her brain screamed she should stay within the relative safety of the crowd. Even though she knew he would take something from her she could not afford to lose once he got her alone.

It was easy to slip away unnoticed from the salon, easy to find the deserted west hall and hide along the deep shadows of the corridor. And very easy to convince herself this was a colossal mistake.

Once out of Theodore's orbit, the swirling thoughts inside her head calmed. She could think clearly. Rationally. She risked scandal with her actions, and she would be wise to hurry along to her room before someone discovered her lurking along the darkened halls and demanded an explanation.

Then she saw it. A kissing bough overhead, one of ten anchored down the hallway. She stared at it for a long moment, considering its presence. Her eyes narrowed in suspicion as her anger, slow to awaken, was roused to such a point that an outlet was necessary.

There were so many of the blasted things in the house. A multitude. They'd grown in number since just yesterday. *There was only one reason for so many...*

A pair of heavily carved dark oak chairs rested against the wall on either side of an equally heavy Elizabethan style buffet chest. Lauren dragged one of the chairs to the middle of the hall and scrambled atop it. By stretching one arm up and holding on to the carved chair back, balanced high on her tiptoes, she could just barely reach the edge of the offending decoration. Once she had it within her grasp, she ripped it free of its moorings so that it fell to the floor.

That task complete, she carefully hopped down, scraping the chair along the plush carpeting to the next bough. It would take some time to remove all ten of the things. How many could she do before Theodore arrived?

She bit back a muffled scream of alarm when a masculine arm hooked her waist

"What do you think you are doing?" Theodore's eyes glittered in the dim light. He held a bowl of lemon ice in his free hand while effortlessly keeping her captive with the other. "Redecorating?"

He'd scared at least five years off her life, but Lauren couldn't let him know that. "Why on earth did I agree to meet you—"

His gaze darted to the bundle of mistletoe laying on the floor and back to her. "You don't know why you agreed?"

She cringed a little; the upward tip of her chin haughty. "No."

"You know why, Lauren." Theodore's grin was slow and wicked.

Lauren's mouth dropped open at his calm, matter-of-fact statement. Before she could voice a horrified denial, Theodore's hand tightened on her upper arm. Tugging her into step beside him, he led her to a huge inset of floor to ceiling windows.

The alcove appeared specifically designed for intimate encounters. Deep and spacious, several persons could stand behind the thick curtains and remain undetected from those passing by. Theodore pushed Lauren against the nook's inside wall where the drape of the curtains hid their bodies from view. Streaming through the glass panes, the full moon reflected off the fresh snowfall. It illuminated the space with the brightness of candlelight.

For reasons Lauren couldn't understand, the bowl of lemon ice still sat palmed in Theodore's large hand, balanced there as he considered her with a slightly furrowed brow.

"I asked you a question yesterday at the pond, and I ask the same question now. Do you still trust me?"

Lauren shook her head to the contrary. It was on the tip of her tongue to tell him precisely why.

"Understandable. So, I will give you a truth in the hopes of changing your mind," he said in a low voice. "But you shall remain very still for me while you listen. No matter what I do. Agreed?"

Curiosity got the better of Lauren. What might this devil admit to? What secret would he reveal? What would he do to her?

A jerky nod of her head indicated her acquiescence.

"Good girl."

His half-smile and those two words sent an unwanted flush of pleasure cascading throughout her body. As she watched, Theodore dipped the spoon into the bowl, brought the dessert to his own mouth, and swallowed. Then, as if in slow motion, he leaned forward until his lips brushed Lauren's.

The sweet tanginess of lemon transferred from him to her. When she inhaled with surprise, he immediately took advantage, his tongue sweeping past the barrier of her teeth and plunging deep.

Lauren moaned, a small sound of distressed arousal escaping her throat that made Theodore draw back. Closing his eyes, he rested his forehead against hers, took a deep breath, and let it out in a small woosh.

"I hated what our fathers did to us, Lauren. Hated it. And I hated deceiving you."

CHAPTER 9

*L*auren's heart seized with the ring of truth in his words. Still, she remained silent.

"For months, my father and yours manipulated our future. Although, once I laid eyes on you, mine was entwined with yours regardless of their plans. It still is, Lauren. Don't you believe that?"

Theodore placed a forefinger beneath her chin and tipped until she had no choice but to look into his eyes. He contemplated her, his expression so serious it left her feeling splintered and yet, somehow complete. "They wanted us together. But the only thing that matters is us and what we want. I know what I want, Lauren. Do you? Do you know what you want?"

She couldn't answer, not when everything in the little alcove was topsy-turvy and the blood in her veins beat in time with the cadence of his voice. If not for the wall against her back, she would have swayed in an unsteady rhythm of desire and uncertainty.

Theodore's finger trailed from her chin, down her neck, to the mounds of flesh straining against the boundaries of her gown. While she stood frozen in paralyzed delight, he loosened the ribbons of the bodice then breached the prison of the corset and her undergarments with relative ease.

He did not stop until she was bare to him and the lick of the silvery moonlight. She did not struggle, held captive by something wild and wicked.

The lemon ice was now little more than a tangy, sweet slush. Watching her intently, Theodore slowly and deliberately dipped the china vessel so the liquid drizzled out.

It dripped across her collarbone, painting the voluptuous, upper curves of her breasts where they swelled above the corset, and finally gilded the tips of her nipples. Theodore placed the empty bowl aside, his hands now free to grip her waist and hold her in place.

Lauren gasped at the sensation, shivering as the icy stream trailed over her heated flesh. Hearing the sound, Theodore growled deep in his throat, bent his head, and chased every rivulet with the scorch of his tongue.

"I want you, my wild, sweet Lauren. I want your fire. Your bite. Your passion. Everything." The words were murmured against her skin, his lips moving over her, tasting and nipping every exposed piece he could find. The furnace of his mouth closed over the tip of her breast, his tongue swirling about the hardened peak like a lick of flame, contrasting exquisitely with the frost of the lemon ice. "I cannot get enough of you."

She should have pushed him away, but for some reason, her hands clasped his head tighter to her, her fingers raking through the thick waves of his hair. A satisfied, yet unfulfilled moan trembled in her chest as Theodore's teeth captured, then gently rolled her nipple. The sharp nip that chased it made her heart nearly explode.

"Theo… Theo, please…" Her whisper was mindless. She did not know what she begged for, but Theodore did.

"Yes, love. Yes. I'll please you… I shall devote my life to pleasing you." With leisurely wantonness, he trailed kisses to her other breast, lavishing the same attention and dedication upon it until she writhed, helpless in his arms.

"What do you think happened here?"

"It looks like a kissing bough fell and someone tried to repair it. Stupid buggers left the chair in the middle of the corridor, didn't they?"

The unexpectedness of two male voices in the hallway nearly sent Lauren into a panic. She froze in place, her hands stilling in Theodore's hair as she registered the fact two other people stood on the other side of the thick velvet curtain.

Theodore's head raised, his eyebrow quirking high as he recognized the danger of their predicament.

"Too lazy to fetch a ladder, I suppose," one of the men offered.

"Here, I'll fix it."

"Leave it for morning," the first one said in a bored manner. "After all, the downstairs maids are responsible for that. I say we tell Mister Collins and let him handle it."

"At least we can move the chair back."

Raising a finger to his lips, Theodore made a "shh" signal then, with his other hand, lightly pinched Lauren's nipple into a stiff peak of arousal. When it seemed she might cry out from the onslaught, he brushed his lips over hers and slyly whispered, "If we are caught like this, you in my arms like this, your breasts exposed like this, and my mouth exploring you like this, you can be damned sure I shall have you as my wife before the sun sets tomorrow. So be still, my darling, else you make that particular dream come true."

Then he fully claimed her mouth, lashing his tongue at hers as if daring her to expose their hiding place.

While the two servants went about setting the chair in its rightful place and discussed how much trouble the downstairs maids might be in, Theodore pressed his advantage and Lauren kept her silence. Her head became muddled, so dazed by the swirl of emotions he evoked that she forgot why she fought being his. He kissed her so voraciously, so tenderly, and so completely that Lauren wasn't sure if there was a good reason *not* to allow him his way.

Between kisses, he nipped and licked her flesh, soothing one instant and setting her afire the next. He shifted his body as well, pushing between her knees, forcing her legs wider until one large muscular thigh thrust between her own.

There was something terribly primal and basic about that. Something that made Lauren push against the stone-like hardness of his limbs. Something that made her rub against him, searching for relief for the unsettling sensation flowing through her body. Something that made her want to never let him go.

"That's it, my darling," Theodore crooned, devouring the sensitive area behind her ear. "Whatever you want, I will give you..."

One huge hand curled around her throat, urging her chin heavenward so more of the tender flesh was exposed. He sucked and bit the smooth column of her neck with that one hand controlling her breath while the other molded her breast to fit his palm, tweaking the nipple until it pebbled almost painfully, sending Lauren down a fathomless vortex of lust.

Her body rocked back and forth, using Theodore's silken steel muscles as an instrument to send lighting sparks of excruciating pleasure twirling along every nerve ending. She was so *close* to an amazing discovery. Pressure built inside her veins. Inside her bones. Her blood. Between her thighs, behind the thickness of her skirts and her flimsy undergarments, it was there. *There.*

Theodore ground harder against her, his growl reverberating until it echoed in her head. A whimper of need, of confusion, of want and frustration fluttered between her lips.

A plaintive, desperate cry for release.

Theodore responded with quicksilver speed. One moment

his hand was on her breast, the next it was up and under her skirts. His leg eased away; his palm replaced it. The heat of him burned through her undergarments. The unyielding pressure as he pressed exactly where she needed him was blissfully exquisite, his hand cupping her sex until she thought she might dissolve like a sugar cube dropped in hot tea.

The hand around her neck tightened the slightest bit, but she wasn't frightened. If anything, she felt more secure as he held her in place. A crazy thought flitted through her mind at that moment and was gone the next instant.

His hands, so strong, so hard and so tender, kept her anchored to the world and would be there to gather her and make her whole if she flew apart.

She *needed* those hands to fill the empty spaces inside her.

"Come for me, Lauren," Theodore commanded roughly. "Come for me and give me your heart."

A firm revolution of his wrist, and Lauren melted, the sensation so overwhelming and unexpected she grew dizzy. The quickness of the orgasm, her first by another's hand, obliterated anything before it. Every splinter of ecstasy was painful, true, and addictive.

She wanted more.

Theodore immediately swallowed the cry hovering on her lips, his mouth consuming hers with an animal-like intensity. It seemed that he kissed her forever, guiding her through the heights of the climax, slipping in and out of the pulsating pleasure of the waves, and finally allowing her to drown in the giddy, dreamy aftermath of the descent.

When it was over, when she was boneless and complacent, Theodore gently withdrew his hand from beneath her skirt.

He tucked her body back into her corset, tightened the bodice ribbons, straightened the elbow-length gloves she wore, and smoothed stray tendrils of hair behind her ears.

Lauren watched him silently, allowing him to move her as he

wished as if she were a boneless doll. There was no hope for her at that moment, anyway. After that jaw-dropping, earthshattering experience, she could hardly string two words together to form a sentence.

Once he finished putting her to rights, Theodore gave Lauren a crooked smile.

"I'm afraid there is no way to hide the stain."

Glancing down, Lauren saw the slight discoloration on her dress caused by the lemon ice. Only then did she register the faint dampness seeping through the fabric. "Oh. That's unfortunate."

She still trembled from the pleasure he'd given her, little tremors rippling up and outward from her sex to the ends of her toes and fingertips. To her own ears, she sounded drugged, her voice slow and husky.

A sinful glimmer danced in Theodore's eyes when they settled on her bosom. "I wasn't thinking clearly before…"

Lauren's gaze was helplessly drawn to Theodore's firm, plush lips. *Just moments ago, those lips were on my breasts. His mouth was on mine. His hand was beneath my skirts, and he was…*

"Lauren." Theodore snaked an arm around her waist, pulling her close. "Go on to your room. Tell the maid you spilled your dessert if she asks, and if she doesn't ask, then all the better." Kissing her softly, he released her with a chuckle. "I'll renew my assault tomorrow, and you can continue fighting my efforts if you like."

Pulling the alcove curtain back, he checked the corridor for unwanted visitors. "Based on your actions earlier, I don't doubt you will still resist." He allowed Lauren to slip past, calling after her in a lowered voice as she hurried away, "But should I catch you standing in a chair again, you won't like the consequences."

～

LAUREN ENTERED her room almost as if in a trance. She didn't even see Anne until she rose from a chair near the fireplace. The maid was waiting for her.

"Here, milady." Anne began unlacing Lauren's gown, clucking with disapproval when she spied the stain on the bodice. "I hope it's not ruined."

"Perhaps it's not." Lauren sighed as the maid pulled the dress over her head in a flounce of satin and ruffles and then helped her out of the corset. A nightgown of soft muslin encompassed her body next, the ribbons at the neck made of silk. Lauren tied those herself then sat at the maple vanity table. She watched Anne in the mirror draw pins from the coiled mass of her gold-sparked brown hair, the intricate design allowed to unwind in a shimmering waterfall down her back.

She groaned in relief as the pressure from the hairstyle eased. Anne began pulling a boar-bristle brush through the straight locks, from crown to the ends landing just above the nip of her waist.

The rhythmic tugging was relaxing, to the point Lauren put aside the incident with Theodore. For a few moments, at least.

"How is Ollie? Is he feeling better?"

"Oh, yes, milady. Asking for something to eat other than broth." Anne hummed a tune beneath her breath as she worked. "He should be up and about tomorrow or the next, I think."

"That's wonderful news." Silence loomed. Lauren picked at the blue forget me knot flowers stitched on the nightgown's sleeves. "Anne, may I ask you a question?"

"Surely, milady."

"Which room does Lord Hawthorne occupy?"

The motion of the brush stilled then began again. Lauren knew she'd shocked Anne, but it couldn't be helped.

"It is down the corridor, milady."

"But do you know precisely the room?" Lauren nudged.

Anne frowned. "You can't mean to go to him, milady. You might be seen… and your reputation would be ruined."

Lauren's lips pressed together. She'd not made up her mind when it came to Theodore Hawthorne. She only knew an odd restlessness flowed through her blood, irritating her with its presence. It calmed when the earl was around, but that in itself was maddening because his very appearance agitated her senses. She wanted to both slap him and kiss him, and she hated herself for the conflict.

"I don't know what I mean to do. But when I decide, will you help me?" Lauren caught Anne's hand, holding it against her shoulder, trapping the young woman's eyes in the mirror's reflection. "When the time comes, Anne, will you do as I ask? Please. As my friend, and not as my employee. In return, I vow I will help you and Ollie in any way necessary. If you wish to marry or acquire your own cottage, I can—"

Anne laughed softly, patting Lauren's hand with her own. "Here now, milady. There's no need for all that. Of course, I will help you. I always will. It doesn't matter much what you might do for me, or for Ollie. I'll do it because you are a kind, decent person. You deserve happiness, milady, and if it is with Lord Hawthorne, all the better. That man is right bonny to look at."

CHAPTER 10

Theodore spent yet another restless night tormented by visions of his skittish fiancée'.

For Christ's sake, he'd not had a decent night's sleep since the day he'd laid eyes on the little vixen he'd soon claim for a wife. While engaged, he'd fantasized of the day she would become his. During their estrangement, he'd dreamed and plotted on winning her back. Now he faced the difficult challenge of making it happen.

It all culminated in what could only be described as agitated slumber.

Why Lauren allowed him those liberties in the alcove was a mystery he could not unravel. How her flesh possessed a flavor sweeter than sugar was even more mystifying. The urge to sink to his knees, lift her skirts, and place his mouth between her thighs had nearly overwhelmed him. He wanted the taste of her in his mouth, on his tongue, in his blood. Only the knowledge he might frighten her with such boldness kept him from plundering her treasures like a starving pirate long lost at sea.

It was nearly noon before Theodore emerged from his room, exhausted and irritable from lack of sleep. Making his way downstairs, he yawned, cursing for not having his valet ring for more coffee. Another cup or two might have erased his ill mood.

Near the rear of the manor home was the largest drawing room. It overlooked the west gardens, and for this morning, it was the gathering spot for Lady Penelope and the other ladies. Their laughter and feminine voices drew Theodore like a moth to flame, for he knew with a certainty he'd find his prey among the lovely flowers assembled there.

Peeking around the door jamb, he saw Penelope presiding over several small tables around which ladies congregated. They were studiously engaged in the construction of delicate cones made from swatches of wallpaper. His gaze skipped over the women until he located the one he sought.

The most gorgeous rose in the garden.

"She is stunning," George Settleton said from just behind him.

Theodore gave Lauren a lingering glance then turned to his host. "That she is. As is your own lovely wife."

George grinned and clapped a hand on Theodore's shoulder, drawing him away from the door. "Both are beautiful and too damn smart for their own good. A word of warning, Hawthorne, you may notice decorations have been depleted in certain areas of the manor."

Theodore tilted his head, genuinely confused. "What the devil are you talking about?"

"The, ah, kissing balls you talked Penelope into hanging everywhere. I know she was to keep your arrangement a secret; however, I insisted she tell me what the hell was going on. The blasted stuff is all over the place."

Shoulders lifting in a shrug, Theodore glanced around the area where they stood. The drawing room's doorway was missing a bough, but the ceiling was sufficiently draped and decorated much like the west corridor. "I think it makes the place rather festive."

"I believe Lauren is aware of your subterfuge."

"Why do you say that?"

"She may be removing the decorations on her own. Just wanted you to be aware." Laughter edged George's words.

"I appreciate it, Settleton." Theodore rubbed his chin. The little minx. He should have known she might discover his ploy and take active measures to counteract it. He couldn't help the tiny smile that lifted his lips.

"Lady Lauren is certainly a headstrong and intelligent young lady. A worthy opponent for any man brave enough to match wits against. No doubt you are up for the task, Hawthorne."

"I hope to do more than match wits. My goal is to regain her heart, if the truth be known. If it requires every bit of mistletoe in your forests to accomplish that, then that is how it must be."

THE WEATHER TURNED RATHER GLOOMY, with snow flurries darkening the skies by mid-afternoon. No one dared venture outside, and guests were finding ways to occupy themselves within the great house.

Several ladies gathered in the South Parlor with their sewing, while some couples took over the library for a variety of games suitable for mixed company. Seeking her out, Theodore was immensely glad Lauren had no interest in playing Blind-man's Bluff. Or even worse, charades.

Instead, he found her in the main salon. Thankfully, she was alone, admiring the paper cones crafted the day before and placed strategically on the Christmas tree's branches. It seemed she was rearranging them, tucking them deeper within the tree itself and fluffing the pine needles.

With her back turned, Theodore admired the loveliness of

her form—the delicate shape of her shoulders, the tiny indentation of her waist, and the graceful flare of her hips. Her heavy and demure coil of hair rested at the nape of her neck, and within him came the burning desire to see her unbound and naked in his bed. He could not deny he wished to see her heart unfettered as well, laid bare before him.

"Such clever decorations." His boots clicking on the parquet floor startled Lauren.

As she looked back at him over one shoulder, her face flushed almost guiltily. Then her attention returned to straightening a paper cone. "Yes. They are surprisingly easy to make." She regained her composure rather quickly, adding with a tiny smirk, "Perhaps you should have joined us yesterday morning instead of lurking about the doorway."

Theodore stalked closer, the snap of flames in the fireplace an ominous accompaniment to his footsteps. When he stood beside her, his finger swept a stray tendril of hair that had escaped from her coiffure back behind her ear. "Perhaps your maid should use more pins to tame your locks."

Lauren bristled. "The taming of anything on my person is hardly your concern, Lord Hawthorne."

A smile briefly lifted Theodore's lips, heat flickering to life in every nerve ending of his body. "After the intimacies we shared, how shall we ever return to the use of formal titles? It's impossible, my love."

For a fraction of a moment, Theodore saw pain cross Lauren's features before her eyes shot daggers. "You insist on inane titles in its place?"

Theodore frowned. "But you are my love. How many times must I tell you this?"

Her cheeks glowed even pinker, her eyes the stormy grey of the sea during a hurricane. "What occurred between us was a mistake. It should have never happened, and it won't again."

Theodore slanted her glance. "A mistake? Lauren, you cannot comprehend just how perfect we are together. Not being together is the mistake." His voice lowered. It was full of challenge and understanding. "You should know I won't give up so easily."

With a mutter of aggravation, she pushed past him, but he caught her arm, pulling her against him.

"Oh!" Lauren's fists immediately planted themselves in the middle of his chest, her breath escaping in a heated sigh.

"You have the most annoying habit of running away whenever I get too close. Unfortunately for you, it only incites me to chase you all the more." An arm slipped around Lauren's waist, resulting in a crinkling sound. Theodore's brow rose high. "What is that noise?"

"I don't know what you are talking about." Lauren chewed her bottom lip, attempting to jerk away. "Let me go—"

He spied it then, a bit of greenery and white berries peeking from the edge of her gown. "What do you have hidden in your gown?" Using his free hand, he ran his fingers along the neckline's lace trim.

"Stop!" Lauren squeaked in alarm, grabbing at his fingers, but Theodore would not be denied. Holding her tighter, he scooped inside the bodice and encountered multiple sprigs of mistletoe.

"What the hell—" Pulling the greenery free of her bodice, Theodore stared at it, then at her. "Is there more?"

"No, you wretched, horrible man! Now, let me go!"

"Lauren." His voice remained calm, but the thread of authority it contained would have a grown man shaking in his boots. "Is there more? Because I will search you myself if I must."

"Oh! The devil take you, Theodore Hawthorne!" Lauren cried, fishing inside her dress and tugging out two pieces of the plant.

Taking them from her while still maintaining his grip on her waist, Theodore glanced about the room.

"Where have you hidden the rest of it?"

Lauren's jaw tightened before waving a hand at the Christmas tree. "I was tucking pieces of it into the tree when you came in."

Her determination in outwitting him was both amusing and frustrating. Theodore could not decide which might win out in this situation. "Just where did this particular kissing bough come from?"

For a moment, it seemed she wouldn't answer, but then her chin tilted toward the fireplace. "Above the mantle," she said, the faintest sneer of rebellion evident in her words.

"And how did you manage pulling it down this time?" Theodore inquired, his gaze taking in the height of the area in question. He could see the spot she'd torn it down from.

"By using a chair like any intelligent person would."

"You persist in placing yourself in danger," Theodore mused, rubbing a thumb over her delicate collarbone and the angry scratch already welting there.

"And you persist in making it your business," she shot back.

"Oh, but it is my business. If you were harmed as a result of our arrangement, I'd find it most upsetting."

"Then cease this madness," Lauren argued. "There's no need for subterfuge."

"Ah. Then you'll kiss me willingly?" Theodore pounced on her statement, enjoying their verbal sparring. It was curiously a bit like foreplay, and he enjoyed these interactions with her.

Lauren's eyes sparked with temper. "You know that's not what I meant."

Theodore chuckled, tipping her chin with his forefinger, so she had no choice but to meet his gaze.

He looked his fill of her, took in her flushed cheeks, the quickened rise and fall of her chest. The soft parting of her lips, so full and pink. She was aroused by the closeness of their bodies and perhaps by their heated conversation as well, which was good because he felt the same. If truth be known, he was going mad for her.

"My dearest Lauren, you are a constant delight. Come with me now. I want to prove something to you."

She gave him a look filled with alarm, her body trembling within the circle of his embrace.

"Did you not prove matters before, Hawthorne?"

"You require additional convincing, it seems," he responded lazily.

"It's not necessary." Lauren's voice strengthened. "What more could you do that wasn't done last time?"

Theodore smiled. "You won't know unless you come with me. Aren't you the least bit curious to know?"

"These attempts at coercion are wasted ones. Besides, if your intent is merely to accost me in a shadowy alcove, you've already done that. You'll need to do better."

Theodore's head dipped until his forehead touched hers. He waited there a moment, then moved until his lips rested against her ear.

His words were raspy, slivers of desire escaping his throat as he bared his lust, and there was no mistaking her shiver of response. "I shall do better. Because Lauren, my intent is to place my mouth between those pretty, silken thighs of yours. For you, I shall lick and bite your tender flesh until you forget your own name. Then I'll begin in earnest until you are screaming mine. Now, come with me, darling, so I may prove my point."

CHAPTER 11

*L*auren gripped Theodore's sleeve, although if the reason was to push him away or pull him close, she wasn't sure. She was saved from the arduous task of decision making by the unmistakable approach of others from the corridor.

Theodore nipped her ear with his sharp teeth and let her slip from his arms. While she quickly placed a respectable distance between them, rubbing the lobe of her ear with shaky fingers, the earl gave her an unrepentant grin. Between his fingers, he twirled the mistletoe taken from the bodice of her gown.

"There you are, Lady Lauren," Lord Sanderson exclaimed, entering the salon with Lord Jenkins at his side and Lady Emma Whitestone trailing close behind. "A group of us are embarking on a frivolous game of Hide and Seek to while away the afternoon. Would you care to join us?"

Theodore's brows snapped together as Lauren stood silent.

Emma stepped forward. She was a quiet thing, very pretty and possessing a warm smile. "Do say yes. It seems like such fun, but we need more ladies if we are to do things properly."

"You're just who we need," Lord Jenkins chimed in.

"Yes, just who we need." Sanderson glanced at the mistletoe in Theodore's hands, and a faint scowl darkened his face.

A heavy silence permeated the salon as Sanderson poured himself a glass of whiskey from the bar service.

"What if I should join your silly child's game?" Theodore stalked toward Sanderson until he'd placed himself between the young lord and Lauren. "Would it upset your delicate ratio of men to women?"

Sanderson's eyes widened before he regained his composure. "Of course not, Hawthorne. We would, of course, enlist another lady to join the fun." He tilted his glass toward Theodore with a smile. "Lady Melanie indicated interest if you decided to play. We would be evenly matched in that case."

Lauren stiffened. She had no intention of playing anything with that woman involved, but if Theodore wanted to run around the mansion hiding in cupboards and darkened corners hoping a lady might grope him, then he was welcome to it.

"Sounds intriguing," Theodore drawled, rocking on his heels. A satisfied expression flitted across his features as his gaze slid to Lauren, gaging her reaction to his next statement. "Perhaps it's best you do go along, Lauren. Lady Emma has obviously never played this game and doesn't realize the damage to her reputation when the wrong participant finds her."

Lady Emma frowned. "I can take care of myself, my lord, but it would be lovely if you and Lady Lauren joined us."

Theodore waved a hand at the girl without bothering a glance at her. "Of course, you can take care of yourself. I did not mean to imply otherwise."

Giving the girl a pointed look, Lauren tried conveying the level of concern she instantly felt. "Such games can be rather outrageous, Lady Emma. Do you have anyone else you can partner with?"

"I see no harm in playing alone," the girl returned stubbornly.

Theodore's winter blue eyes narrowed on Lauren. "What do you say then, Lauren? Shall we?"

Lauren lifted an eyebrow. She wasn't so naïve as to mistake Theodore's secret intent. He wanted to find *her* alone... somewhere he could continue this assault on her heart unimpeded. He'd declared warfare, and oddly enough, she was eager to reengage in battle.

"Yes, we shall." Lauren nearly laughed out loud at the surprise in Theodore's eyes. Her words twisted to fit their situation, reminding him he'd concealed the truth for so long. "I've no skill with this particular game, but maybe I'll be as good at hiding as some of the expert players."

THEY GATHERED with approximately eight others in the library. Melanie was there, and Lauren gritted her teeth when the lady's eyes lit up with pleasure to see Theodore. It went against everything in her nature, but she sidled closer to him. Glancing down at her, he simply arched a brow, quirked a knowing smile, and tucked her hand into the crook of his elbow.

As the rules of the game were explained, amidst much giggling and excited conversations, Theodore leaned down and whispered in Lauren's ear.

"Go directly to your room. I shall meet you there."

When she stiffened in silent protest, Lauren felt Theodore's grin even though she couldn't see it. His breath was responsible for the chills racing up and down her spine.

"Do you really want Sanderson to find you?" he inquired softly. "Now, you will go to your room, won't you?"

She nodded, casting her eyes downward when she noticed Melanie staring at the two of them.

"You will send your maid to Lady Penelope with a message. You've developed a sudden headache and decided to rest for the afternoon," he instructed further, and Lauren nodded again.

Theodore moved away, hands clasped behind his back, silently waiting until Sanderson finished explaining how things would go.

"I'm afraid my aversion to parlor games prohibits me from participating after all," Theodore tsked softly. "Forgive me if my absence throws the ratio into chaos."

The women murmured in disappointment. Melanie's eyes narrowed with suspicion, focused on Lauren and Theodore.

"It will still be great fun, I think!" Emma exclaimed, clapping her hands.

"Of course, we wish you would reconsider, Hawthorne, but your feelings on the matter are noted." Sanderson was almost gleeful. "While it is little more than a nursery game, there's something to be said for the thrill of the hunt."

Lauren frowned at Sanderson's choice of words, discomforted at the thought of being pursued through the halls of her cousin's home. Her gaze caught and held with Theodore's for a brief instance. The bright gleam of excitement she saw in the blue depths sent anticipation zinging through her veins. There was no doubt, if the game were conducted on his terms, he'd show no hesitation in hunting her down.

"I'll leave you to it. For what it is worth, if bets were placed on the outcome of this... hunt... my money would most certainly be placed on Lady Emma Whitestone. She seems a most formidable opponent, for all her inexperience." Theodore smiled at the young woman as others tittered and nudged each other. "I do believe she will route you all."

Bowing at the waist to the collective group, he turned to Lauren. Lifting her hand, he pressed a soft kiss upon it, his expression promising much more once they were alone. "I wish you luck in the games and hope I find myself seated beside you at supper tonight. Until then, Lady Lauren."

The game began in earnest.

Lord Sanderson insisted on being the first seeker. The hungry look he wore each time his eyes passed over Lauren was disturbing. That look sent her scurrying through the corridors to the safety of her room the moment his back turned and the count started. Never mind the rules stating private spaces could not be utilized as hiding nooks.

Anne was there, preparing the gown Lauren would wear for supper.

"Good afternoon, milady." Anne's smile was distracted as she smoothed wrinkles from the dark ivory silk. "Is everything all right?"

"Nothing but a headache, Anne. You can put the gown away. I think I'll have a tray sent up for my supper." In her own ears, Lauren thought she stuttered over the words, but Anne seemed not to notice. "Would you please tell Lady Settleton I won't be down?"

"Certainly. I'll have a pot of tea sent up right now, too. It might help."

"Some brandy as well, if possible."

"I'll have Ollie deliver it, Lady Lauren."

"Thank you, Anne. I'm so glad he is improved. After the brandy and tea are delivered, you may take the rest of the evening for yourself. I'll ring for supper when I'm hungry."

Before long, a pot of tea and a decanter of brandy were delivered to Lauren's room. Ollie ducked his head, discomforted to have his employer inquiring over his health. He was still quite pale, but his cheeks bloomed pink whenever his eye caught

Anne's eye. Their mutual affection was readily apparent and had only strengthened as a result of his sickness. Upon assuring Lauren he was nearly back to normal, he excused himself, and Anne rushed to complete her duties.

After helping her mistress into a pale pink nightdress with a matching robe and pulling the pins from Lauren's hair so it released in a waterfall of richly hued brown silk, Anne departed.

Moving to the fireplace, Lauren sipped her tea. She was understandably nervous, waiting for Theodore's arrival. It had been nearly forty-five minutes since she left the library under the guise of playing hide and seek. Perhaps he had changed his mind. Perhaps he'd only been toying with her.

Perhaps he was detained by Melanie, or someone she had not recognized as a rival. Someone like Lady Emma. She was quite lovely, and Theodore made that rather curious remark about her winning the game. Maybe he was interested in her...

Oh, such nonsense! Lauren chided herself. Theodore was single-minded in his pursuit. How could she believe he might abandon her in favor of another?

Finishing the tea, she set the cup down, glancing at the decanter of brandy. She requested it for Theodore on a whim, but quite honestly, a sip might help calm her nerves.

Calm my nerves for what purpose? What might Theodore do that's not already been done?

The answer to that was sobering. There was much the man could do. Much she secretly longed to experience under his hand. Recalling his scandalous words, the husky lilt of his voice while informing her just where he would place his mouth on her body, sent a shiver through her that had nothing to do with the lingering chill in the room.

A slight noise by the door alerted Lauren that she was no longer alone. Taking a deep breath, she twisted about and found Theodore had entered the room unnoticed.

The earl leaned against the closed door, shoulders flush against its surface, arms folded across his chest. One leg casually crossed before the other with just the toe of a boot touching the hardwood floor. He was the epitome of the sophisticated lord, his dark clothing blending with the shadows of a dreary, winter day and the softly lit room.

"Hawthorne." The tiniest crack appeared in her voice, splintering in the air between them. She swallowed, her hands clenching into fists. Nerves were getting the better of her.

"My love," he replied so softly Lauren strained to hear his words. Her heart thumped wildly when she realized what he'd said, and the truth of that simple statement was overwhelmingly stunning.

He *did* love her. Madly. Completely. Unquestionably. After rejecting him for months, humiliating him with a broken engagement, and forcing him to face almost certain financial ruination, Theodore Hawthorne still loved her in spite of it all. Lauren's eyes burned with sudden tears, tears that were blinked away as quickly as they formed.

For a long moment, they merely stared at one another, a moment when an unspoken vow was made—and accepted.

Eyes glittering with triumphant satisfaction, Theodore pushed off from the door. With one hand, he turned the lock until there was an unmistakable click. His coat was removed, tossed carelessly over the upholstered arm of a nearby chair. All the while, his eyes never strayed from Lauren's, causing her stomach to swoop and dive as if a flock of wrens had invaded her body and taken up residency.

The chiseled lines of his mouth quirked in that cynical half-smile she'd become addicted to, a lock of dark hair tumbling across his brow in a riot of chaos her fingers ached to smooth. He seemed larger in the soft glow of the firelight, even with the lines of his body melting into the shadows. But she wasn't afraid. No, it surely wasn't fear that made her tremble while he stalked her like a lion pursuing its chosen mate.

Once he reached her, Lauren swayed, dizzy with want, with need, and with confusion. How could she surrender to him so easily? So quickly?

She had the answer when his hand lightly threaded through her hair, fingers rubbing the glossy strands as if judging the most luxuriant of fabric. She thought he might pull her immediately to him. Wrap an arm around her and begin kissing her, but she was wrong. He merely caressed the long tresses, winding it about his fingers as one would a spool of ribbon. Trapping her when, secretly, she possessed no desire to escape.

Theodore gave an experimental but gentle tug, a half-smile lifting his lips when Lauren moaned in surprise. Her head lolled with his touch; the muscles of her neck suddenly lax as her senses clouded with pleasure.

"For so long, I've wondered what your hair might look like, unbound like this," he murmured. "It's stunning. So soft. So fluid. It flows like a river of dark honey."

In direct contrast to the abrupt relaxation overtaking her body, Lauren's heart turned helplessly over on itself. Twirled, twisted, and tangled until every nerve ending she possessed was aching and reaching for him. Her hand slid over his corded forearm, fingers contorting in a desperate grasp she hoped would ground her. Why was she suddenly breathless? As though the strings of a corset had been tightened to the point of pain and no amount of air could find its way into her lungs.

She was floating away in a dreamy world, and all that mattered was this man's worship. His adoration. His attention. She wanted to be his everything. Forever.

"Easy, my sweet darling. Easy, now." Theodore's voice was a mix of tender amusement and arousal. Cupping her jaw in one large hand, he gently forced Lauren to meet his gaze, his eyes darkening to an indigo blue that enthralled her. She couldn't look away. She didn't wish to.

His fingers moved to her throat, stroking the slender column almost reverently, tracing the lines of it as she swallowed in reflex. "I've so much pleasure to give you. So much to show you," he whispered, his mouth brushing her ear, tickling it with warmth. "But first, take a breath. That's it. And another. Good girl. Can't have you fainting before I even begin."

CHAPTER 12

God help me, what manner of devilish torture is this? How am I to keep from ravishing her when she's dressed like this?

Theodore stared down at her, grateful that her eyes were momentarily closed so he could drink his fill of the delectable sight she presented. The nightclothes, while not overtly sensuous, were crafted with an eye toward wicked purity. The soft, pale pink of innocence contrasted sharply with the nearly sheer muslin fabric. He never expected finding her dressed in such a manner, much less in a way giving him undeniable access to her slender body.

His blood pounded in his ears. Christ, he could see her nipples through the material. They were just a shade darker than the blush-hued muslin.

He knew what they tasted like, how they felt under his tongue. Sweeter than the first raindrops of spring. Softer than the innermost petals of his garden's first rose.

"Lauren, why are you dressed so?"

Her eyes lifted slowly as if doing so was a struggle. "Your instructions were clear. To say I have retired for the evening."

"Are all your nightclothes designed in such a manner?"

Her brows knitted together. Glancing down, she appeared befuddled by her attire. "How strange."

Theodore lifted her chin with a forefinger, holding her gaze. "What is that, my love?"

Something sad flashed in the silvery depths of Lauren's eyes. "This was part of my wedding trousseau. It must have been packed by mistake."

Her wedding trousseau. Theodore felt his muscles tighten in response. Had their wedding gone as planned, he would have seen Lauren in gowns even more revealing since consulting with the seamstress himself. He would have demanded a private showing of every single article before stripping the last one from her body and tossing her onto their marital bed. They would have enjoyed the pleasures found there for the rest of their lives together. Night after night.

If he could convince her their engagement was still very much a reality, there was still hope for his fantasy to come true.

"It is very lovely, and you are a vision in it," he said softly, hoping she would not become melancholy with the reminder of their botched nuptials. Especially when he was working so desperately at amending the situation.

Lauren met his gaze unflinchingly. "Thank you, Theo." But when she resisted his increasingly tight embrace, he let her go. Her fingers twisted together, a nervous habit.

"Would you care for a brandy? I had some brought up." Her nod toward a table by the fireplace drew Theodore's attention to a tray with a decanter and one glass.

"Yes, but I will pour." Theodore smiled. "One for you, then perhaps a bit more for me."

Only when he pressed the glass into her hand did he realize her body was trembling. Indeed, nearly invisible tremors racked her. Was she frightened of him? Did she regret allowing him entrance to her room? Did she think he might pounce on her and take with no regard for her feelings on the matter?

Frowning, he waited patiently until she swallowed the liquor, choking on the fiery stuff. It trickled out of the corner of her mouth, and she wiped the droplets away with the back of her hand. Another dram was poured, and she drank that down without question, heedful of its burn the second time. The little shivers she exhibited gradually eased away as he so carefully watched her.

He then poured himself a glass, draining it before gathering her into his arms once more. Her body felt more relaxed against him, less tense, but her eyes were still clear as she gazed up at him. The last thing he wanted was an intoxicated fiancée, but clearly, his motivation in giving her the brandy was to help ease her apprehension. It seemed to have worked.

"What is the matter, love?" Theodore's tone held a soothing quality.

"You would have seen me in this nightdress months ago had our marriage taken place as planned. We would be husband and wife right now." Her voice was small and troubled.

"Yes," he agreed. "That's true. I regret not seeing you in it sooner. Do you think it is merely coincidence this garment was included in your belongings? Or that I am here at your cousin's? We have been pushed together once more, darling. For the right reasons this time."

Lauren's brow knit together as she attempted to make sense of his words. "But we're not married. This is wrong."

His hands caressed her shoulders then moved so her jaw was cradled in his palms, his fingers meshing in the silky wealth of her hair. "Nothing about *us* is wrong, do you understand?" he declared fiercely. "I love you, Lauren, so don't dare tell me this is wrong."

The next instant, his mouth crashed down on hers. Not violently or even in punishment, but certainly with a bit of frustration. He wanted her. He wanted her badly. He wanted her to accept the fact their lives were meant to entwine.

The sweet essence of brandy lingered on Lauren's lips. It paled in comparison to the flavor of her mouth when he delved deeper. She tasted of sugared peaches and reluctant desire. Theodore wanted to feast on her until any woman in his life before her was erased.

Without interrupting the kiss, he scooped her up into his arms, swallowing her tiny moan of surprise. The bed was only steps away, and he carefully placed her atop the coverlet, crawling up beside her, never breaking the fusion of their mouths.

Lauren's robe fell open, further exposing her body. There was no hope of resisting the lure of such beauty. Theodore's hand lifted, smoothing the filmy garment away until the sheer gown beneath the robe was revealed.

With a groan, Theodore tore away, breathing heavily. Fascinated, he watched his own hand mold her breast through the fabric, shaping it to fit the span of his palm. Lauren's eyes latched on his while she shivered under the weight of his large body. They fluttered shut as he leaned back down, hovering above her like a beast with a fresh kill.

"Lauren, if I dangled mistletoe over you this very moment, what would you grant me? Another kiss? A truth? Or a favor?" Each choice was punctuated with a heated kiss along the column of her neck, his hand sliding to the hem of the nightgown. It had ridden high when he placed her upon the bed, exposing her long legs. During their kiss, it edged up even further until it lay atop her thighs.

Encountering the bare skin there, Theodore shuddered. Damn. She was smooth as silk, her flesh warm and soft. A whimper escaped her as his fingers skated along until he reached the gentle flare of her hip.

"An answer, darling," he murmured. "Kiss. Truth. Or favor."

"Truth." The admission flew out in a hiss when Theodore nipped the slope of her shoulder. "I—I will give you a truth."

Shifting his weight, he let his fingers dance between her thighs. With deliberate movements, they dipped into the soft wetness there, brushing the delicate button of nerves until her hips lifted to meet his touch. For long, breathless moments, he stroked her. Until she was panting. Writhing. Desperate. Hungry.

"I'm listening, Lauren."

She bit her lip, and Theodore forced back his own groan of lust. She was pulling him under. Drowning him in a sea of desire.

"I want you, Theo. But don't... don't hurt me..." Her answer was the barest of whispers.

"Never." The sudden press of his fingertips against her most sensitive flesh elicited a gasp of pleasure from her lungs. Theodore's heart swelled with tender protectiveness at the frantic sound. God, he wanted to hear that from her lips every night for the rest of his life. "I'd just as soon cut out my own heart."

Lauren hesitated before giving an almost imperceptible nod of surrender. "Then do your worst, Hawthorne."

He smiled at her bravery, gliding his blunt, elegant fingers over her slickened folds again. "Darling, nothing but my best will ever do where you are concerned." Taking her mouth with his again, he kissed and sucked at the plump flesh of her lips until she mimicked his actions.

When he finally pulled back, Theodore was the one who was slightly breathless. Drunk on the sweet taste of her mouth and the damp silkiness of her flesh. "I'll stop the moment you ask it of me, Lauren."

Her fingers coasted over his shoulders, testing the muscles bunched and hidden beneath his shirt. "And if I don't ask?"

"You will." Theodore took her hand, kissed her fingertips, then grasped her other hand so both wrists were easily bound in the circle of his fist.

Her dove-grey eyes dilated slightly when he tugged her arms until they stretched above her head. Displayed and immobile, Lauren trembled beneath him, caught up in the whirlwind of desire.

Bloody hell, how he wanted her. Wanted to fully claim her. Wanted to bind her to him and make her his forever. Wanted to plant his babe in her belly and watch her grow round with the life they created together.

"You are so beautiful, Lauren. My heart aches just to look at you sometimes," he confessed.

In response, Lauren tilted her hips so they bumped against his. Her tongue darted out, moistening full pink lips already parted in anticipation of his mouth descending upon hers. She moaned in delight when he gave in to the invitation, kissing her with a wild roughness that should have terrified her.

"Remember, darling," he whispered between the deep, invasive sweeps of her mouth and the conquering of her soul, "you must stop me when you've had enough or if I take more than I should."

CHAPTER 13

*L*auren was certain of it.

She'd never been kissed so thoroughly. So deeply. So... *intensely.*

Theodore slid a knee between her legs, pressing her open. The upper portion of his thigh brushed against the sensitive tissues of her sex. He was built like a Greek god, the muscles of his leg hard as stone and unyielding against her softness. His actions became increasingly bolder, his fingers gliding over her in sensuous repetition.

The brush of his erection on her leg startled her. The powerful force of it, thick and straining against the confines of his clothing, sent dizzying waves of lust galloping through her veins.

She couldn't breathe. Gulping for air, she struggled to calm herself as he nibbled on her skin and his fingers explored her flesh as he wished.

Would she have the resolution to stop him? Would she even wish to stop him? She couldn't be sure when her willpower was almost nonexistent.

Every time she took a breath, Theodore stole it. Every time

she writhed, he stilled her, the inability to move provoking more flames from deep within her belly. From under her skin. From inside her heart. Until she was consumed and incinerated to dust.

"Yes, that's it, my love," he grated out as she moaned. Still holding her hands in one fist, he gripped her hip with the other. Pushing harder, he lazily guided her movements until she rocked upon his thigh. The encouragement to use his body as though it were an instrument of pleasure spiked her desire past a breaking point.

Pressure gathered. Built. Swirled and sought escape. A mindless, irrational need clawed at her insides. Swelled until she almost sobbed in desperation. She would do anything… *anything*… for him.

"Theodore… Theodore…" Her voice was shaky. High-pitched. Greedy. "Yes. God, yes…"

Before she could fathom his actions, Theodore ripped her gown open. The thin cloth tore easily in his large hands, exposing her body to the chill of the room. But she didn't care, and there was no time to contemplate the loss of the garment. He moved with such graceful swiftness it was startling. His thigh shifted away. In a blatant claim of possession, his body slid down hers. His head dipped lower. His mouth claimed her aching sex and then…

And then heat combined with overwhelming, exquisite sensations. His tongue explored the delicate seam of her womanly core, reverently tracing the plump flesh. Flattening to taste all of her in one long, leisurely swipe, he ended this first assault in a fiercely gentle suckling of the nub hidden behind the soft curls.

Lauren cried out. Agonized delight flooded her, exploding in bursts of color and sensations too intense to comprehend. Releasing her wrists, Theodore now gripped her hips with enough force to bruise the skin. Those large, capable hands slid under her buttocks, holding her aloft as if in sacrifice to ancient gods. His fingers grasped so tight she knew instantly he would devour her with the ferocity of a hungry lion.

"You fucking taste like peaches," Theodore growled, sucking and licking and biting between words. "Come in my mouth again, love. Come again for me."

His tongue speared her flesh, thrusting with such firmness that Lauren began shaking once more as he commanded her body. Disjointed thoughts tumbled in her mind. Was this the residue of the first climax? Or the beginning of a second?

When it finally crashed over her, the glorious intensity was overwhelming. Her world spiraled out of control. Disoriented, Lauren could only weave her fingers through the thick waves of his hair. The silky strands were something to grasp, something tangible in the palm of her hand. She held on for dear life.

But it didn't contain her. It couldn't. She was floating away. Floating on a cloud, somewhere in a twinkling night sky. The threads of her soul and all the lifeless pieces of her life were illuminated. So brightly lit, she wouldn't be able to view her reflection in a mirror come morning. Spreading deep, permeating her vulnerable heart, thunder rumbled through her body. Or maybe it was just his voice, declaring she belonged to him. That he was keeping her.

A storm had come.

And Theodore was the lightning.

Lauren drifted down in a pleasant, hazy fog of awareness.

Theodore still knelt between her thighs, nuzzling her skin, kissing the mound of her womanhood with tender attentiveness. His fingers no longer gripped her so harshly but now coasted over her. Skimming the soft, white flesh of her belly, tracing the lines of her flanks and the quivering expanse of her outer thighs. Sliding his hands to the inside of her legs, he pushed them to spread even wider.

At the stretch of her muscles, Lauren lifted her head, meeting his eyes over the plane of her flat stomach. While his glittered with a mixture of desire and regret, she did not see any indication he would go further than he already had. Disappointment edged away her satisfaction at the realization.

"You should stop me now, Lauren."

The words whispered across her skin where his mouth pressed. Each breath was a little spark from a bigger fire. Each caress a flame waiting to be reignited. Each kiss a promise he could burn her alive again and again, and she would beg him not to stop.

"Why?"

Lust flashed in the blue depths of his gaze at her question. He did not look away as he nipped her hipbone before answering.

"Because soon, I won't be able to stop. Push me away, Lauren, before I do something irrevocable. I don't have the willpower, you see. Not with you." His smile was sad. Lopsided. "I never do with you."

"You haven't any mistletoe," she said. "No justification."

"It doesn't matter. I won't need it. Now, push me away." Even as he harshly instructed her, his fingers were spreading her open again, preparing her for the lush sinfulness of his mouth.

"I—I cannot," Lauren groaned as he thrust two fingers inside her. Hot and probing, his tongue darted out, lapping up the evidence of her arousal. "Theodore, please. Don't stop."

Oh, what was wrong with her that she was eagerly accepting of this? So hungry for him? So desperate for his touch? He had turned her world upside down. Everything was topsy-turvy. To the point she would give him every shilling of her obscenely massive inheritance. "I cannot deny you."

"Lauren, I'm begging you..." His words were frantic, muttered between licks of her flesh. *"Send me away!"*

Still fully dressed in afternoon attire, although minus his coat, Lauren dazedly supposed Theodore resembled some sort of ravaging beast hovering over his prey. How pale she must appear in comparison, her nudity in stark contrast to his dark clothing. She couldn't send him away. Not when he was so hungry for her and she for him.

With customary stubbornness, Lauren shook her head, clutching handfuls of his hair so she could hold him harder against her. Theodore cursed something unintelligible, the heat of his breath searing her flesh.

"Then I will take what is mine, and before I make love to you, I will taste your sweetness once more on my lips." He suckled the sensitive bud between his teeth and gently bit down while thrusting his fingers upward in a curling motion.

Ecstasy, sharp and sweetly exquisite, loomed on the horizon. But this was different from before. This robbed Lauren of breath. Of sanity. Of any resistance.

When Theodore did it again, she quivered in obedient response.

Captured and held prisoner on the precipice of something dangerously, wondrously addictive.

"Theo..." His name escaped her in a helpless, keening cry of pleasure. An answering low growl of satisfaction emanated from Theodore.

BOOM!

It's my heart. Exploding. Can Theodore hear it? He must, for it's so loud... like thunder.

BOOM! BOOM! BOOM!

"Lady Lauren? Are you there? I must speak with you at once. It is imperative."

A man's voice penetrated Lauren's haze of desire, punctuated by someone's fists pounding the door to her rooms. The swelling inside her caught and held, trembling, waiting to be pushed over the edge or allowed to recede. It only needed another thrust of Theodore's fingers, a bite from his sharp teeth, and she'd be flung over the stars and back. Flying without wings.

"What the bloody hell..." Theodore hissed. Lifting his head, he glared in the direction of the door then back to Lauren. His fingers remained curled inside her but had gone motionless now. "Goddamn Sanderson. I will murder the fool before all is said and done."

"Sanderson?" Lauren repeated, blinking rather stupidly.

"Indeed, my dear." Theodore's eyes held a devilish glint. "He's determined to court you, it seems. Shall I allow him to enter? Or should I stay otherwise engaged?" His fingers flexed experimentally, and Lauren melted with a gasp. But the delight was short-lived. He was already withdrawing from her. Rolling from the bed, he stood beside it and gave her a fierce frown.

"Lady Lauren? I know you are there..." Sanderson's insistent voice sliced the air between them. He knocked again, three sharp raps.

"It is men like him your father wished to shield you against." Theodore waved a hand toward the door. "Brash, unthinking, selfish, greedy."

"As were you," Lauren said, sitting up and drawing the tattered edges of her clothing together. The robe, still intact but just as flimsy and delicate as the nightdress, was hurriedly wrapped tightly around her body. "Yet, my father handed me over without a moment's hesitation."

Theodore's eyes narrowed, his gaze almost silver in the shadows. "Yes. He did, and I accepted that gift and responsibility."

"Lady Lauren?" Sanderson sounded almost plaintive. "I'm merely checking on your wellbeing."

Ignoring the man on the other side of the thick, wooden

door, Lauren rose up on her knees upon the mattress. Rather shakily, she reached for Theodore's hand. "What would you do differently now? If given the chance?"

Theodore swallowed hard. His eyes pinned her, gleaming in the shadows of the room. "It's a conversation for another time."

Lauren rubbed her thumb over the back of Theodore's hand. "My father had much to do with my state of unhappiness, I'm afraid. I am only now discovering it is impossible to lay everything at your feet." Looking up, she saw an expression of heartbreak mar his features. She wanted to fold him into her arms. Forgive him for the many nights she cried, her heart breaking because she thought he'd meant to use her.

"You may place anything you desire into my care, Lauren. Even yourself." Theodore breathed. "I will always handle you as though you are crafted of the finest porcelain. Do you not understand yet that you are my most precious treasure?"

Sanderson pounded again and incredibly, tried the doorknob. It jiggled with a soft clinking sound as the lock was tested.

"I thought I might keep you company, my dear," the man declared, his voice muffled by the oak door. "Or I could be of assistance in massaging your temples should your headache still persist. I'm quite good with my hands. Won't you let me in?"

Theodore gave Lauren a look filled with astonished fury. "I will break every bone in his body if he dares touch you."

Lauren grimaced, bounding off the bed before he could stop her. "That's hardly a sentiment in keeping with the Christmas spirit, Theo," she exclaimed over her shoulder while moving toward the door. "One moment, while I make matters clear to Lord Sanderson."

"Lauren, don't open that door."

In response, she stuck her tongue out then sidestepped him with a giggle when he lunged for her. Guessing he might make a second attempt, she dashed across the room, nimbly evading capture while Theodore swore under his breath.

She flung open the door. With a scant second to spare, Theodore removed himself from Sanderson's line of sight, his hands and teeth clenched, ready to tear the other gentleman limb from limb.

Sanderson noticeably gulped at the vision of loveliness before him. For a long moment, it seemed he could not speak. His gaze roamed over Lauren, taking in the wealth of unbound hair, her flushed cheeks, and the mussed condition of her garments.

Lauren's eyebrow arched in what she hoped was a haughty expression of displeasure. "You disturb my rest, sir."

"I—uh—I hoped to assist," he stuttered. His eyes fixed on her bosom, partly exposed where the robe gaped. The gown beneath and its ragged edges, torn by Theodore's eager hands, peeked through.

Abruptly mindful of her scandalous appearance, Lauren frowned and gripped the flimsy robe closer to her chest. Perhaps she should have considered this before confronting the very persistent Sanderson.

"It is completely unnecessary. Please do not bother yourself on my behalf any further." She made to close the door. "Goodnight."

Shaking himself from his trance, Sanderson grabbed the edge of the door with his hand. His foot wedged in the opening. "It would be of mutual benefit, I assure you. And pleasure."

A strangled growl emanated from somewhere deeper in the room.

Lauren covered the unmistakable sound with a clearing of her throat. "You flatter me; however, this behavior is the height of impropriety, Lord Sanderson. You must go."

"But I..." Inexplicably, his sentence trailed off.

Lauren puzzled over that until it became glaringly apparent. A jolt of horror rocked her. Sanderson had spied the gentleman's coat tossed haphazardly over the chair. His gaze fixed upon it.

Stunned silence ruled for a moment. Lauren held her breath for what felt like an eternity before Sanderson eased his foot away. "Do forgive me, Lady Lauren. It is my wish you are feeling much improved tomorrow." Removing his hand from the door's edge, he gave a stiff bow.

"I'm sure I will. Good night, my lord."

"Yes, erm, goodnight." The man hurriedly stepped back, practically fleeing down the hall.

Lauren chewed her bottom lip as she quietly shut the door and relocked it. For a moment, she rested her head against the cool wood. How much harm would it cause her reputation if Sanderson bandied about that there was a man's afternoon coat in her room? Perhaps she could bluff her way through it. Say it had been left there by mistake previously during a completely guiltless visit.

"I warned you not to open that bloody door," Theodore muttered into the curve of her neck. Arms wrapped around her tight, pulling her hard against his muscular body. His warm, broad chest burned her spine through their clothes, and Lauren fought the urge to sink into him.

"I worried he might break it down," she whispered back.

"If he had, he'd find himself answering to a brace of my pistols at dawn." He spun her around, cupping her jaw within the palm of his hand. "He saw my coat."

"He can't possibly know that it is yours."

Theodore's smile was indulgent. "Who else would dare enter your rooms?"

Lauren had no answer for that. She gazed mutely up at him while he brushed her cheek with the knuckle of his forefinger.

"You are so innocent in these matters, my dear," he stated with an exasperated sigh. "If he hasn't informed half of the guests by tomorrow morning, I would be very much surprised."

Leaving her slumped against the door, Theodore made his way over to the table holding the brandy. After pouring himself a hefty serving and downing it in one gulp, he took up his coat. Instead of shrugging into the garment, the garment was tossed over his arm. His intent was abundantly clear.

"You are leaving?" Lauren rushed to his side, gripping his arm. "But why?"

Theodore's hand slid into her hair, fingers gently caressing the nape of her neck. Drawing her close, he pressed a kiss to her lips.

Lauren tasted the brandy, sweet and heady, felt the warmth of his mouth, overwhelming and intoxicating, and she swayed against him.

"You know very well why. Because I would take more." His mouth brushed hers. "We both know you would not stop me. We cannot be trusted with each other, wouldn't you agree? This is for the best, darling. Until you agree you will be my wife, it must be this way." One more fleeting kiss and he was pulling away from her. "These are but tiny glimpses of heaven that whet our appetites, and because we are equally starved for each other, *that* is why I must go."

CHAPTER 14

Theodore entered the library, heaving a deep breath of relief when he saw it was empty. On a sideboard in the corner sat a tray of liquor, and he poured himself a whiskey.

Sinking into a deep chair, he rubbed a hand across his forehead.

Lord, what an afternoon it had been. He still felt Lauren's warm body as if he held her in his arms. But far worse, he could still taste her. Even through the burn of the whiskey, he tasted her.

From his pocket, he withdrew a bit of the mistletoe he now carried everywhere. Twirling it between forefinger and thumb, he considered his plan. A frown spread across his face.

It had proven more difficult than he'd thought, this winning of Lauren's heart. Once on the verge of claiming the prize, morals now hijacked his goal. He still couldn't quite understand what had happened or why it happened.

He left her when she practically begged him to stay. Pushed her away while she pulled him closer. Ignored her lips when every nerve cell in his body shouted he should ravage her mouth.

Only five days remained before the wager was officially over. He should call an end to things. Seduction may have been an unwise choice, especially now that his efforts had borne fruit.

Maybe his greed, his pride, had gotten the best of him, turning him into someone like Sanderson. He'd stolen Lauren's choices away. Made it all about what *he* wanted.

Bloody hell if he'd hadn't made an unholy mess of things.

The door to the library creaked open, and Lord Settleton strolled in. He wore a smile, though there was a hardness in his eyes.

"Ah, there you are, Hawthorne," George said with a telling forced joviality. "I thought you had retired for the evening. At least, that's what Sanderson said."

Theodore stiffened. *Already running with the rumor. This will turn out badly.* "What else did he say?" He slowly rotated the glass in his hand.

"Very little." There was a period of silence as George poured himself a drink. Taking a seat in the chair opposite of Theodore's, his brow arched. "Why? Should he have said more?"

"It is of no matter." Theodore stared at the other man. A man he considered his friend. A man who also happened to be Lauren's closest male relative.

"It is the greatest of matters," George returned calmly. "But you already know that, don't you?"

Tipping his head back, Theodore let out a frustrated sigh directed at the coffered ceiling. When next he met George's calm gaze, his jaw ached from clenching, and his hands curled into fists. "Has he spread the tale any further than your ears?"

"Not that I am aware. Only to myself, I think. I told Penelope, of course. She is with Lauren now, relaying the events. There were no promises from Sanderson that he would keep this confidential. He appeared ready to burst at the seams when relating what he saw."

"For all intents, Lauren and I are still engaged," Theodore ground out. "It greatly dilutes any associated scandal."

"Many do not believe your engagement to be intact. That includes your betrothed, my friend."

Theodore scowled. "Damn Sanderson, anyway. The man is hell-bent on stealing her away for himself."

"Yes. It appears so." George cocked his head. "What shall you do?"

"I am inclined to silence the man permanently. But as I am currently enjoying your hospitality, and it is the holiday season, I shall restrain such murderous inclinations. Besides, other guests would probably not appreciate bloodshed during such a festive time."

Swallowing the remnants of the glass, Theodore rose to his feet. He smiled grimly at his soon to be cousin-in-law. "I shall try stifling Lord Sanderson, although ultimately this decision as to how Lauren and I proceed shall be hers to make. I'm a realist. I know our options, although she will most likely disagree with me."

"What choice shall she have?"

Theodore's heart twisted a bit because he wondered if Lauren would choose either scenario he planned to put forth. "A scandal before Christmas, or an elopement. Either way, we are bound to shock society."

~

"My mother?" Lauren stared at Penelope over the tea tray her cousin had personally delivered to her room. "She asked if you would invite Theodore, knowing you had already extended me an invitation? I don't understand."

"Neither did I, at first. But then Lady Hawthorne requested the same, that I invite the earl if I was assured of your attendance." Penelope squeezed Lauren's hand. "I'm sorry, my dear. I swore I would not reveal the machinations which led to both of you being here, but at this point, I owe you the truth of the matter."

Lauren chewed her bottom lip, deep in thought. She actually was not surprised. Mother had asked several times if she had any intentions of forgiving Theodore. Lauren evaded giving an answer, knowing the fondness Mother held for the earl. It seemed she and Theodore's mother had conspired together in the effort to bring Lauren and Theodore together once more.

The question was, did it upset her as much as it should have? Was it the same as the scheming their fathers undertook?

The truth of the matter was it didn't feel the same. At least, not when Lauren carefully considered it. No, it rather seemed more a gesture of hopeless romanticism. Two mothers desperate for their children to fall back in love.

"I think they mean well," Penelope sighed.

"Theo said something earlier. Perhaps he was trying to tell me, but I paid no heed to his words."

"It is conflicting, isn't it?" Her cousin laughed softly. "On one hand, it's sweet. On the other, so very meddlesome. At least, Lord Hawthorne is prey to their interference along with you."

Lauren twirled the sash of the robe around her finger. It was a fresh garment, matching the new nightdress she wore beneath it. When Theodore departed earlier, she immediately changed clothes, hiding the ruined gown deep in her traveling chest. "I cannot blame him this time for the actions of our parents."

Penelope took a sip of tea. "What shall you do now?"

"I must think upon it. If scandal would touch only myself, it would not concern me so much. But I've no wish for Mother or Lady Hawthorne to be impacted by our actions. I fought marriage based on the concept of being sold for my inheritance. This is different. I believe Theo truly loves me, and I—I love him. The principles for my breaking off the engagement haven't changed, however. It was a betrayal of trust. I'm still over-coming that."

"It is a hard thing to forgive. But if ever a man deserved it, perhaps Lord Hawthorne is that man. His devotion to his family, to the care of his mother and his estates and those dependent upon him, is beyond reproach. He includes you in that circle, Lauren. Even after the death of your father, he has not stopped looking after you and your mother. George told me of Hawthorne's oversight of your barrister. He was greatly concerned that your investments were handled properly, that your inheritance was secure. Even if you never saw him again, he would look after you because he promised your father he would."

Lauren's eyes welled with tears. Theodore's actions were so pure and struck her heart so deeply, they left her breathless. How selfish she had been in her anger. How stingy in her fury. The one person she could truly rely on for advice and comfort, and she'd rejected him. Cast him aside.

"Penelope, I wonder if you would do something for me?"

"Anything, my dear."

"Will you take me to Hawthorne's rooms and grant me access? He and I have much to discuss before this night is over."

Penelope grinned. "That can be arranged. Anything else you might require?"

Lauren thought about it for a moment before a wicked smile curved her lovely lips.

"As a matter of fact, there is. Can you procure a bit of mistletoe for me?"

CHAPTER 15

Theodore found Lord Sanderson in the east parlor just before supper.

The man was alone, a glass of whiskey in one hand, his brow scrunched into a frown. Visibly startled at seeing Theodore, he took a long gulp of the glass's contents.

Closing the pocket doors behind him with a soft click, Theodore advanced. There was no mistaking the sheen of sweat on the other man's brow. Good. This might be easier to accomplish than previously thought. It certainly smoothed the path when one's adversary was more than slightly intimidated.

"A word, if you don't mind, Sanderson."

"It—ah—it is near the time supper will be announced. We should not tarry, Hawthorne."

Theodore's lips twisted slightly. "Our absence will not be remarked upon, least of all by our hosts."

Sanderson's hands trembled, his gaze touching on Theodore's black suit. "Is there something you wish to discuss?"

Theodore poured himself a glass of whiskey as well, his eyes steady on the other man. Earlier, he had retired to his room, readying himself for supper by donning the required formal attire. "There are several matters, actually. But one rises above all others in terms of importance. You see, this particular subject is very dear to me. An extension of myself and one I will defend to my dying breath."

Sanderson swallowed. "I understand your meaning, sir."

With a tilt of his head, Theodore stalked closer. "Do you? Perhaps that is true." He finally stood almost toe-to-toe with Sanderson, calmly regarding him as a trickle of sweat eased a path down the other man's temple. "I prefer there to be no mistake when it comes to my expectations, so I will clearly state my purpose and the consequences if I am disappointed in any way." Theodore's stare flickered. "Another?"

"P-Pardon?" Sanderson stuttered.

"Another whiskey?" Theodore gestured at his empty glass.

"No."

"Good. Now I can get right to the point." Taking another sip of his whiskey, Theodore pinned the man with a dangerous glare. "Whatever you saw, or believe you saw in Lady Lauren's rooms, dies a death this very instant. It will not be spoken of nor bandied about for the rumor mills to feast upon, and it most certainly will not serve as kindling for revenge after she rejected you. I am saying this in the clearest way possible, so there is no misunderstanding. Lady Lauren is my fiancée, soon to be my wife. Insulting her is an insult to me. You, or any man foolish enough to test the depths of my devotion, will face my wrath."

Sanderson had grown pale while Theodore spoke and, very carefully, he set his empty glass down on an elaborately carved occasional table.

"I've told no one—"

"Ah, that's not entirely true, is it?" Theodore murmured.

"I mentioned it to Lord Settleton just in case there was any confusion."

"I will not allow scandal to touch Lady Lauren. Whatever you believe you saw will not be spoken of from this moment on.

Should word reach my ears that this warning has been ignored, I shall be left with no choice, Lord Sanderson. I *will* handle matters in the deadliest of fashions. With my bare hands, if necessary, and odds are I will enjoy it beyond the realms of decency. I would do this for the honor of the woman I love and for that of my family." Theodore's voice dropped to a husky, threatening growl. His eyes glittered with an icy blue blood lust that made the other man shudder with trepidation. "Do we understand one another?"

"Perfectly, Lord Hawthorne. Perfectly."

Theodore's teeth flashed in a satisfied, predatory grin. "Then let us drink to wise decisions and a long life. I, for one, am relieved I don't have to kill you."

THEODORE CALMLY SAT THROUGH DINNER, amused by Sanderson's attempts at diverting attention away from the fact they entered the dining room together. The man stuttered and fumbled, but not once did he mention Lauren's name, not even when Lord Jenkins pointedly asked if he'd had any luck during the afternoon games.

Lady Emma was seated beside him, something he had not expected. She gave him a friendly smile while pointedly ignoring Lady Melanie's angry glares and Lord Jenkins' hungry glances.

Penelope, seated at one end of the long table, merely nodded when Theodore caught her eye. Aware she'd spoken with Lauren, he wondered if she was vexed with him following their private conversation and curious what may have been divulged.

"Lord Hawthorne, may I confide something?" Lady Emma hesitantly touched his sleeve as the first course of consommé was served.

Theodore turned his attention to the petite brunette. "Of course."

"You were correct in your assessment regarding the dangers of playing certain games." She blushed, her hand immediately returning to her lap.

"What do you mean, Lady Emma?" Theodore took a sip of his sherry, noting Emma's flush deepened even as her eyes sparked with anger.

"I chose my hiding place today very carefully. So carefully, I was able to go undetected. Because of that, I overheard one of my pursuers describe to another gentleman of his acquaintance his intentions once he found me." Her fists clenched in her lap. "At first, I was furious as they were obviously not following the rules of the game as explained to the rest of us. It seemed the men were hunting in pairs, assisting each other until a lady was located. I realize how naïve I was to ignore your warning. You were trying to help, and I foolishly dismissed your advice."

Theodore's gut tightened. Had the games gone too far? Would the holiday be darkened by selfish lust and a belief this was only a bit of harmless fun? "What happened? Were you hurt?"

"No, no. I stayed in place until they moved away. I then decided I would return to my room until it was time to come down for dinner."

Relief trickled through Theodore. He smiled at her. "Given the opportunity to bet, I would have still wagered on you to win it all."

Emma grinned back, her dark eyes dancing. "I would have, too." Glancing around the table, she located Lord Sanderson. "I've noticed Lord Sanderson is very careful not to mention Lady Lauren's name, and she is not here for dinner. I hope she is well… that she… that she did not suffer some manner of upset."

Theodore sank back in his chair, considering this turn of events. Although he had efficiently muzzled Sanderson, others might mention Lauren's absence during the course of the game. Especially since Sanderson had disappeared as well. It would insinuate something scandalous in nature had taken place, and that would not be abided.

"Lady Lauren was in perfectly good health when last I saw her," he said softly.

Emma's head tilted. "Yes. We had similar ideas when it came to hiding spots. I'm not sure what drove her out of hers, but together we quickly decided we would return to our rooms. Nothing seemed amiss when we parted ways, but perhaps something occurred after."

"You left the game together?" Theodore did not bother hiding his surprise.

Emma intently considered him for a long moment. "Of course, we did. You understand, don't you?"

He knew full well Lauren had gone straight to her rooms. Because she followed his directive, she had not taken part in any aspect of the game.

Emma was providing herself and Lauren a means of protecting their reputations.

"Of course," he nodded. "That was very kind of you."

Emma took a sip of sherry before returning to the business of eating her soup. "The kindness extended on behalf of Lady Lauren was my honor, I assure you. Should you see her before I do, will you give her my thanks?"

"I certainly will. And Lady Emma, like myself, Lauren never forgets the actions of a friend."

CHAPTER 16

*L*auren fidgeted with the scalloped hem of her nightgown.

Sitting in the middle of the bed, she glanced around Theodore's room. It was spacious and tidily kept, his valet obviously very meticulous in his efforts to keep things orderly. Because of Penelope's intervention, at least she could be sure his servant would not interrupt them tonight.

Picking up the sprig of mistletoe her cousin handed her just as she was leaving, Lauren smiled. It seemed fitting it be used as a means of showing Theodore she'd decided she would become his wife.

But how much longer would she have to wait for him to arrive? The mantle clock had struck eleven-thirty, meaning dinner had ended over an hour ago. Even with the requisite cigars and brandies following the meal, he should have retired by now.

"You are being unreasonable," Lauren muttered to herself. "He'll be along soon enough."

As if on cue, the doorknob turned, and Lauren hurriedly straightened her posture, smoothing a hand over her hair. The mistletoe, clutched so fiercely between her fingers, was in immediate danger of being mangled.

Theodore entered the room, his attention on removing his coat. He did this as though in deep thought, his back to the bed. Tossing the garment over a nearby chair, he made his way to the fireplace and poured himself a brandy.

Staring in the flames of the fire, he drank while Lauren watched his form, backlit by the glow and gilded as if in gold. Her heart contracted, squeezing painfully tight as she realized how very much she loved him.

Leaning an arm against the mantle, Theodore sipped until the brandy was gone. He twirled the glass absently.

Lauren bit her bottom lip. What was he thinking? Was he thinking of her and their time spent together earlier? Was he wondering when he might see her again? Or was he plotting how he might convince her to marry him? With a deep sigh, she took fate into her own hands.

"Will you stare into the fire all night?"

Theodore stiffened in response to her soft question, his back straightening although his head remained bowed. His hand tightened around the glass before he slowly placed it upon the mantle.

"What are you doing here, love?" He kept his back to her, and Lauren shivered at the dark, dangerous quality of his voice. If he was surprised at discovering her in his room, he did not show it. He sounded… tense. Cautious. Aroused.

"I wish to finish our conversation."

"Most definitely not the ideal time or place, Lauren. How did you get in here, anyway?"

"Penelope." Lauren studied him, taking in every nuance of his body and its reaction to her words. "I do not plan on leaving this room until we have settled this matter between us, Theo. Won't you look at me?"

A shuddering breath escaped him. "I don't dare."

Lauren swallowed. "Why? Have you changed your mind about me? About us?" The last word came out almost as a sob.

Theodore let out a harsh laugh. "Changed my mind? Far from it, love. It is taking all the willpower I possess not to ravish you."

"Please, Theo. Come here to me." Perhaps if she pleaded, he would relent.

"St. Simon's Cross, Lauren—" The curse tumbled from him. His hands clenched into fists against his thighs, shoulders rounding with the effort to keep from whirling about and pouncing on her. "This is dangerous. Dangerous and foolish, and I don't know what the hell your cousin is thinking by allowing you in here..."

"I shall ask the same question I posed earlier today. What would you do differently if you could? Would you tell me what our fathers had done?"

Theodore slowly turned, seeking Lauren out and finding her in his bed. His eyes pinned her in place. The twin orbs glowed in the soft light cast by the fire, so bright and so fierce, Lauren thought they could be rare sapphires.

She wondered what he thought of her, sitting as she was in the middle of the rumpled sheets, a night rail of dark blue silk barely concealing her body. Did he find her desirable? Did he think her plain brown hair softy and shiny? Was her skin too pale for his tastes? Were her lips full and pink enough that he dreamt of them?

"Dear God," he choked out, finally. "You are a vision. A gift I do not deserve. Are you truly here?"

Lauren's heart pounded as though it were a wild herd of horses set free from captivity. With a tremulous sigh, she reached for him.

He came forward hesitantly until he stood beside the bed. Enfolding her hand into his larger one, he stared down at her, his eyes roaming over every curve and line of her body. She flushed, warming from his gaze and the incredible heat of his hand.

"Theo?"

He shook himself, reaching out with his free hand to trace the plumpness of her lips with a forefinger.

"I would tell you the truth of the matter," he admitted in a low voice. "That my father was dying, our fortunes were long depleted, and I alone was responsible for the estates and the care of my mother. My lofty title was of no use when creditors refused to extend finances. My father and Lord Kendall believed it best for all involved if you did not know the details behind our engagement. To my shame, I followed their directives because I wanted you so much, but it was wrong. I was wrong. I should have told you from the very start. If I had, we would have started our marriage with honesty and trust."

"Father knew my stubbornness. The idea of being sold for a title and safety repulsed me."

"It may have suited other purposes financially, but *we* fell in love first, Lauren. Before anything else, there's that, and it's the truth. No matter what else you might think, above all else, I loved you first."

A tear tracked down Lauren's cheek. She swiped it away. "I believe you, Theo."

Theodore's eyes closed, a momentary selfishness where he appeared to be thanking some higher being. When his gaze locked on hers again, it was with fierce protectiveness. "Now, you must return to your room. We shall call for Penelope to escort you..."

"I'm not going anywhere."

His hand tightened on hers, their fingers entwined. Leaning down, he murmured against her ear, "I threatened a man's life tonight for you, Lauren. Promised I would tear him apart with my bare hands if he so much as uttered your name in a way that displeased me. Made sure he understood I would take great pleasure in it if he dares slander your honor. Lady Emma, in protecting her own reputation, linked her retreat during the games with your absence. I'll not have those actions erased now." His eyes roamed her features with undisguised hunger. "There is no other option. You must go because I can't protect you if you stay, darling. Not from myself. Not from what I want to do with you."

Lauren held up the mistletoe, her manner solemn. "I do not wish for protection. I wish to be kissed and held. I wish you…"

A hand clapped over her mouth, cutting off her words. "For the love of God, Lauren," he choked out. "Have mercy."

In response, she nipped his palm.

Theodore let out a sharp hiss, his hand snatching away.

"If there is mistletoe, you must kiss me, Theodore. Are those not the rules you put in place?" Lauren's eyes flashed with silver fire. "Or do they only matter when you are the one enforcing them?"

"Damnit, I'm trying to save you from yourself… and from me."

"I don't want to be saved. If dying by fire is the only way to prove…" Lauren shot back.

"There are a thousand ways to die," Theodore interrupted with a growl. "Having torn myself away from you once, I'm discovering it kills me to do so again."

"I choose to die in your arms. By your kiss. Hearing you say I am yours and you are mine. I will die saying I love you." Her words flowed out in a rush, her hand keeping his prisoner when he might have pulled away. "Theodore, don't push me away now when I am giving you everything I have. I am surrendering."

His features softened, his gaze turning molten. "Never, darling. Never surrender. I will not have you on your knees for me. I will not have you as anything other than what you are— fierce, stubborn, loyal, and smart enough to make me see how wrong I've been."

Sinking onto the bed, Theodore took her by the shoulders, his long fingers gently caressing her flesh as he stared at her. "Do you truly mean what you said? That you love me?"

"I've never stopped." Lauren inched closer, reveling in the heat of his body. Intoxicating and lavish, it radiated from him in waves. It left her drowsy and yet embroiled in a heightened sense of awareness. The broad expanse of his chest beckoned for her fingers, calling for exploration, and the palms of her hands twitched with restless hunger, ready to smooth across the muscles hidden beneath the white cambric shirt. "I've always loved you. I always will."

Theodore slid his hands down her arms until both her hands were captured in his, the mistletoe crushed. Leaning forward, his forehead touched hers as he swore a hoarse vow.

"I love you, Lauren. I want to marry you. Take care of you. Give you half a dozen babies, all blessed with your gorgeous eyes, and watch them with you as they grow up. I want to squabble with you about insignificant things, then make amends by covering you head to toe with kisses. I want to grow old and grey with you, knowing we'll spend eternity together side by side."

Lauren laughed, a little sob escaping at the same time. "Yes, Theodore. I want that, too. All that and more."

"Anything for you, my love. Anything." He kissed the tip of her nose. "I have one secret to confess, one I should have revealed sooner. Our mothers conspired to bring us together here. For different reasons than our fathers, I think, but a conspiracy nonetheless. Does this change how you feel about us?"

"I already know, and I cannot fault them. They love us both very much and only want to see us happy." Her lips parted as she gazed up at him, and without even realizing it, she willed him to kiss her. To take her mouth and shape it to his own. To own her breath and breathe his into her lungs. To claim her soul, body, and heart.

"I hope you agree an elopement is in our immediate future." He kissed Lauren so softly it wrung a moan from deep within her chest. "If I could marry you this very moment, I would."

"Will you kiss me instead, Theo? Will you make love to me?"

A wicked grin curved Theodore's lips until he resembled a hungry wolf. "When you are in truth my wife, we shall make love until we both collapse."

"I do not want to wait. I want you now."

"Unwise, my love." He chuckled at her eagerness, and Lauren wanted to stomp her foot that he wasn't taking her seriously.

"Make love to me tonight and marry me tomorrow," she demanded. "The mistletoe is supposed to make you compliant."

Sobering, Theodore smoothed a stray wasp of hair from her brow and tucked it behind her ear. "I am easily commanded by you. Always. But I won't dishonor you before we wed."

"And if I demand a truth, a favor, or a kiss?"

"I would grant all three." Cupping her stubborn chin, he brushed his mouth over hers.

"Then let us begin with a favor," Lauren murmured. "Remove your clothing."

CHAPTER 17

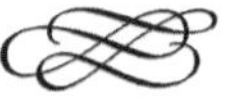

Theodore shook his head.

"I'll not take your virginity here, and not before we are man and wife."

Lauren's head tilted. "A momentary bit of pain. A spot of blood. I am already yours in my heart. The time and place matters little to me with the exception that it be here and now, Theo. If you worry that you may hurt me, you do so needlessly. I know what to expect."

"So, now you attempt to ease my apprehensions," he mused. "How can you possibly know the full extent of what I will do if your demands are met?"

A tiny smile lifted the corners of her lips. "Mother provided some details during the time we were engaged. Penelope answered even more of my questions earlier tonight."

Theodore was slightly stunned Lauren's cousin would knowingly contribute to her deflowering under the viscount's roof. But then again, Penelope and George had their own rather scandalous beginning to their marriage. After carrying on a secret love affair under the very nose of Penelope's uninterested fiancé and her parents, the two of them had eloped to Gretna Green.

Lauren sensed his wavering resoluteness. Moving closer, she brought her arms up so they looped around his neck. "This is what I want, Theo. It is what you want, too." Her eyes, so warmly grey like the summer sun flashing on water, held his until he wondered if he might drown in their depths. "After everything, after all these months apart, isn't our love worth what *we* want?"

Her fingers caressed his nape, lightly grazing the flesh, sifting through the strands of his hair, their mouths so close that his breath caught and mingled with hers. Theodore could not conceal the shudder of desire that raced through his body.

"Lauren…"

His shaky whisper was answer enough. With aching sweetness, Lauren closed the distance between them, her lips touching his gently at first and then with a growing hunger. Her tongue slipped into shy contact with his, retreated, then returned until Theodore met her plea, their mouths mating in an ancient dance.

It was a kiss so passionate, so heart-stopping and possessive, and so beautifully raw, it was quite possible that time stood still.

When the earth resumed its rotation, Theodore discovered his shirt had been unbuttoned by quick, nimble fingers, and warm, feminine hands were smoothing the fabric off his shoulders.

He never released her mouth while tearing the shirt free from his body. Once that was accomplished, his hands gripped Lauren's tiny waist, pulling her against him. Crushing her to his broad chest so he could feel her firm, high breasts burning his skin even through the thin, satin nightdress.

"I'll be gentle," he murmured when he finally took a breath, kissing the slender column of her neck, delighting in the scent of roses and the taste that was uniquely hers. "I'll try, at least."

"I know you will. I'm not afraid." She angled her chin higher, letting him devour her as he liked, gasping when he moved lower and nipped her shoulder. When he chuckled at her response, she turned her head and licked the spot just below his ear before taking an earlobe between her teeth and worrying it gently.

"Little minx," he groaned in surprise at her playfulness. "You'll be the death of me. You know that, don't you?"

Lauren laughed softly, running her hands over his chest as if awed by the sharply chiseled muscles rippling beneath the skin. "You are so wide. So hard and strong."

The words were followed by soft lips skating over the flesh her hands just touched, hovering for a brief second above his flat, disc-like nipples. Then... a lick, a languid swirling of her tongue across the turgid flesh, an experimental taste before her teeth closed over each one in turn to give a teasing bite.

The slight pinch of pain only heightened Theodore's arousal, to the point he thought he might explode with the need to bury himself deep inside her.

"Christ, Lauren," he choked out while her hands maneuvered even lower until they rested on the button placket of his trousers.

"The rest of your clothes, Theo. Shouldn't they be removed for this to work properly?"

She blinked up at him, innocent and flushed, her eyes dark silver with arousal, and all that silky brown hair flowing around her shoulders. The shadowy vee of her breasts, decadently exhibited by the nightdress's neckline, demanded he run his tongue over the exposed silky flesh. But he wanted more than just that little sliver. He wanted all of her. Now.

Rising from the bed, he quickly stripped free of his remaining garments and boots and returned to her. Intending to tug the gown over her head, he reached for the hem, but she grabbed his hands, halting his motion.

"Wait."

Theodore froze. He recognized the unsure quality of her voice. The slight tremor of fear it contained. Her eyes were glued to the area of his groin.

Dread seized his heart and bottomed out in his stomach.

"My love... I'm sorry. I've frightened you with my impatience, my roughness—"

Lauren gave a shaky laugh. "No, wait. I only want—I want to look at you." Her gaze traveled his body, from neck to thigh and all gorgeous slabs, edges, hollows, and bulges in between. "Oh, Theo. You are so beautiful. So... amazing."

Her eyes lifted to meet his, shy but bold. Curious, but hesitant. Because this might not be acceptable behavior between a man and woman, and she was new to all of this, and only he could teach her.

"A truth, Theo." At his nod, Lauren's lips parted slightly with anticipation. She licked them, a slow swipe of her tongue passing over the pouting top lip first, the lush bottom one last. "May I touch you? As you touch me? Do you... want me to touch you?"

Theodore's eyes closed in a silent bid for strength. For willpower. For divine intervention because, God help him, he felt capable of ravishing her like a pillaging thief. "You are killing me, Lauren. I may burn up in flames on this very spot, but yes, you may touch me, however you like. Whenever you like. I am yours. You are mine. Remember that."

She assessed his form again, lingering in certain areas, and damn if he didn't harden all the more because of it.

Then, very softly, she instructed, "Lie back upon the pillows."

Lauren's pulse raced like mad.

For all her outward calm, she trembled like a leaf as Theodore followed her instructions without a hint of hesitation.

When he was in place as requested, she faltered, suddenly unsure of her next move. Because there was so much of Theodore to admire… to salivate over. To worship and adore. He sprawled across the bed, propped by stuffed pillows like a magnificent warlord. Great expanses of gleaming skin lay bare before her, waiting to be explored however she wished.

There were his shoulders to begin with. Wide and defined with angular edges and thick tendons leading to biceps that flexed and bunched with muscles when he moved his arms above his head, clasping his hands tight at the base of his neck. She'd already discovered the mysterious planes of his chest and the way he quivered the tiniest bit when she touched him.

Her determination to conquer his willpower led to the intriguing roadmap of ribs and the blocks of muscles that demarcated his abdomen. How intriguing to find a whispery fine and yet somehow coarse trail of black hair that extended below his navel, reaching downward to a nest of the same consistency between his magnificently sturdy thighs.

And then there was…

Oh, goodness…

Stretching boldly toward the ceiling, thick as a half dozen candlesticks bundled together and crowned with a glistening dewdrop of moisture, Theodore's manhood waited for her to do as she willed. It appeared both soft and rock-solid, an impossible combination in Lauren's opinion. The flared head, which she thought oddly resembled a mushroom of sorts, could almost be considered pillow-like. In fact, if it wasn't for the fact it sat atop a long, thick rod that looked inflexible, she would say that particular bit was definitely non-threatening.

Below all that were two round parcels of flesh. Smoothly plump, they apparently served as the base for all the important bits and pieces, nestled like jewels in the mound of curling black hair.

Lauren studied it all carefully, intent on not missing a single detail, especially admiring the narrowness of Theodore's hips and the trimness of his waist. Even his outer thighs swelled with muscles as they gave way to the firm globes of his buttocks. All in all, he was beautifully created. An exquisite masterpiece of the male physique.

"Lauren." Theodore's voice was low, shaky as if he might cry or shout. He stared at the ceiling as if he couldn't bear to even look at her. "In the name of all that is holy... please. Do something. *Anything.*"

The desperation in his tone almost frightened her. "I'm unsure where to touch you first," she replied apologetically. "Or what I should call the parts I do touch."

His gaze immediately lowered, finding and latching on hers, burning with such intensity the orbs resembled twin flames in pools of deep ocean blue. Tight with unnamed emotion, his jaw clenched as words were forced through his teeth. "My cock. Touch my cock. The head of it... fuck... I'm begging you..."

Tugging at her bottom lip with her teeth, keeping her eyes on his, from her kneeling position beside him on the bed, Lauren reached out. Very lightly, afraid of hurting him for he sounded in such agony, she traced the slit marking the crown of his penis with her forefinger.

"G-goddamnnn..."

The moan rumbled from Theodore's chest, and Lauren almost snatched her hand away. But his next word moved her even closer.

"More."

With a deep breath, she did as he asked, experimentally making a circle with her finger and thumb and sliding it over the mushroom-shaped head of his cock. She was rewarded by a groan of appreciation. Encouraged, the rest of her fingers splayed wide and slid down his length, although she couldn't encircle him completely.

Upon reaching the twin smooth spheres below, she cupped them briefly in her palm, amazed by their softness, before gliding back up the hard shaft to the top. Increased moisture leaked from the slit now, and as her palm traveled up, Theodore's hips rocked skyward as well, following the motion almost mindlessly.

Instinctively, Lauren shifted closer and wrapped both hands around him, causing Theodore to arch into her grip.

"Your skin feels like velvet," she marveled in a whisper as Theodore thrust into her hands. "How can you be so hard and yet so incredibly soft? I wonder if you will feel like this inside me. Like burning iron wrapped in velvet."

"Christ above. Don't say things like that, love."

Lauren swallowed hard, staring at the massive hunk of flesh in her hands. "I'm sorry. I don't know what is proper…"

He huffed out an agonized groan, his body straining toward her when the motion of her hands faltered.

"I only mean that you might cause a reaction you're not expecting…" he breathed out a hurried explanation. "I swear I don't mind, darling."

Lauren was relieved she'd not done anything wrong. Still hesitant, she resumed stroking him, noting how the skin of his shaft seemed to grow tighter around the hardness it contained. "This is all right, then? To keep touching you this way?"

"Yes… for God's sake, don't stop. Slide your hand up and then down just like that. Grip me harder…"

Lauren followed the instructions, intent on learning what she might do best in pleasing him.

When she rubbed her thumb first over the flared head, then the slit while her hand breached the top of him again and again, Theodore groaned his approval.

A fine sheen of sweat broke out on his brow, glistening over pectoral muscles and the flexing biceps so easily seen as he kept his hands locked behind his head. His head was thrown back on the pillows, his hair a ruffled mass of waves giving him the decadent look of an exotic sultan.

Lauren could not stop staring at him in all his masculine beauty. Her eyes darted from his face, where he now bit his own lip to contain his moans, over the massive width of his chest, heaving with unsteady breaths, and down to where her palms cradled his manhood.

She watched him as her hands pleasured him, fascinated by the savagery of his expression, the desperation she glimpsed in the stark, hard planes of his features. He stared at her before shutting his eyes in helpless surrender to the erotic moment.

Lauren found herself so entranced by his reaction; she was overwhelmed. She wanted more. More of him. More of this. More of it all. She wanted him in her bloodstream, coursing through her veins, and the only way of gaining such immediate gratification was to have his flesh inside her somehow.

Without thought, she bent low over his hips, her lips lightly brushing the crown of his erection before she pushed more of him into her mouth.

"Oh, fuck..." Another strangled curse that might have been her name followed that, exhaled on a fiery groan. Theodore jerked inside her mouth. The head of his shaft, the only part she had engulfed, twitched with shudders of delight. His hands, previously self-restrained, now plunged into her hair, burying themselves, gripping tight to keep her where she was. All ten of his fingers pressed against her scalp, reminders she'd placed herself in his hands, and now, he might not let her go.

But she was a willing prisoner. Innocent on how to proceed in such matters, but willing all the same. Her mouth opened more, and Theodore surged forward with a feral grunt. Suddenly, her hair was looped around his hands, an abundance of shiny rope he could use to control her.

The very idea excited her.

The thought she was driving him mad with lust spiked her own desires. She moaned, and because he held her in place, preventing any movement, it heightened the need to move all the more.

Tugging against his grip, her head bobbed up then down in slight increments. Her lips pressed firmly to create suction around him. Her tongue, since she didn't know quite what to do with it, swirled around the part of him inside her mouth, her hands still covering the rest of him.

The taste of him, salty and musky sweet, seeped through her senses. He was both hard and soft inside her mouth. Velvet wrapped steel indeed, but hotter than she ever imagined. It was as though all the blood in his body, all the warmth inside him, now lay encapsulated within the hard shaft inside her mouth.

His hands tightened. Beneath her upper body, which had come into contact with his to the point she was sprawled over him, his thighs trembled. His abdomen contracted, throwing muscles into sharp relief.

With a sudden, jerking motion, Theodore urged Lauren to take more of him, his grip dictating the speed and depth of his thrusts. His motions were almost reluctant. Forceful, but reluctant in a way that indicated he couldn't help himself, and he hated that fact.

Suddenly understanding how he held onto a thin thread of control, Lauren softened. She instinctively opened further, her throat muscles objecting but the willingness to please overriding her body's startled protest.

Glancing up at that moment, she discovered Theodore watching his cock glide in and out of her mouth. There was both pained delight and savage triumph in his wintery blue eyes. And shining through it all was his love for her.

"Enough..."

The word came hissed between Theodore's teeth as he

abruptly lifted her off him, his cock popping free with a soft noise. For a split second, Lauren thought he was angry before he crushed her against his chest and fused their mouths together.

He kissed her for a long time, worshipping her lips, tracing her tongue with his, sucking it deep inside his own mouth until she repeated the gesture. Finally, when she was panting and breathless again, he drew back, his expression fiercely protective as he studied her.

"You've bewitched me, Lauren Georgianna Kendall. I love you beyond the depths of reason. I'm going to make you mine before sanity has a chance to stop me."

CHAPTER 18

$\mathcal{B}$efore Lauren could react, Theodore had her flipped on to her back.

She blinked up at him, stunned. Where a moment ago she held a position of power, he now loomed over her prone body.

"You've driven me mad; you realize that, don't you?"

"Yes," she replied simply. She wasn't sorry for it either. She wanted him mad with desire for an eternity.

"I'll spend the rest of my life making you happy." Kissing a path down her neck, Theodore took the edge of the gown in his hand, pulling it up and over her head in one smooth motion. "There. Let me see all of your beauty. How gorgeous you are, Lauren. How lucky I am."

Lauren trembled beneath him, nervous, and yet, somehow proud he was seeing her this way.

"Each time I see you like this shall be as the first," he murmured. "I've no doubt you will always take my breath away. That you will finally be mine is a dream come true."

Theodore, hot, naked and oh, so heavy, pressed against her body. His skin was scorching. Lauren felt as if she were being branded by the contact. The coarse hair of his chest abraded her sensitive nipples into aching peaks. The muscled slabs of his thighs push hers apart, and the rigid length of his cock brushed over her clit. When she whimpered from the overstimulation of sensations, his breath feathered her lips in a soothing kiss.

Lauren touched his shoulders, fingers coasting lightly over his skin, and Theodore bowed his head as a tamed lion would. Accepting her touch and desperate for more, he moved into a position that would result in the loss of her virginity.

"It will hurt, I'm told." Theodore sounded pained, and a glimmer of regret lurked in his eyes.

"I know." Even faced with that truth, Lauren's stomach still quivered with anticipation.

"Spread your legs for me, my brave girl."

She did, then waited for him to surge inside her.

But he held there against her instead for a long moment as if deciding what to do. When he'd determined she had relaxed, he reached down and grasped hold of his shaft. Fisting it at the base, he brushed it over her softest parts.

"You are so wet for me. So wet and warm. Ready for me to take you. To slide inside you." Theodore maneuvered his cock up and down in time with his words. Soon, he was dripping with evidence of her arousal, and Lauren could not help but bite her lip. If she thought the head of his shaft felt like velvet iron upon her lips, it was nothing less than silk-wrapped stone as it skimmed the opening of her body. She moaned in delight as nerve endings she never knew existed fired to life. Her legs opened wider, fingers clutching his shoulders and nails digging in to create half-moon marks in his skin.

The pleasure was unimaginable; waves of ecstasy overtook her as Theodore expertly coaxed her to a trembling, quaking, roiling climax simply by using the head of his cock.

"Dear God… Theodore," she cried out. "Yes. Yes, yes."

"Now you are truly ready. Open for me. Let me inside." Theodore pushed his way in, and Lauren gasped as her body allowed it. "Breathe, Lauren. Breathe and concentrate on the pleasure."

It stung. Even with her body's moisture, it hurt. There was a feeling of pressure along with the burning intrusion, and taking a deep breath did not seem it would help at all. But something inside her wanted him to continue. She did not want him to stop. Pulling him closer, she willed her body to soften to the invasion, to allow him to plunder and take whatever he wanted.

His cock slid in slowly, breaching every inch of her until he settled against the thin shield of her virtue.

"Hold on to me, darling. Hold on tight," Theodore's whisper fluttered against her ear.

Tears sprang to Lauren's eyes, and with a jerk of her head, her grip tightened. Braced on his forearms, Theodore brushed a kiss on her forehead.

"Only pleasure after this, my love. I swear it."

Then he surged forward, swallowing her surprised gasp with a branding kiss that lit her soul on fire. Only when he was completely sheathed did he finally pause.

That sliver of time, an eternity of heartbeats shared between them, was everything all at once. Affirmation she'd been right in allowing herself to fall for him again.

Her body melted and accepted. Clasped and contracted. Forgot and forgave. Her heart stuttered and started again, stronger and stronger until she thought she could soar to the moon. This, *this* was where she'd been meant to be all along.

How foolish I've been.

When her body had adjusted and molded around his deep inside her, Theodore's hand found hers. Their fingers meshed together, their palms touching.

"I'm going to move now. Before I go insane with my need for you." Staring intently at her, he moved her hand high above her head. His other gripped the flesh of her hip. "Stop me if I hurt you."

"Yes, Theodore."

"Promise me."

"I-I will."

He began moving in a slow, gentle glide that rocked Lauren's body. She felt the same ricocheting pangs of pleasure as before, but they were muted for some odd reason. Perhaps it was an overabundance of sensations? She couldn't be sure.

Theodore was attentive to the nuances of her body, to her expression, and his mood was somber as he plunged with growing urgency. His hands tightened, keeping hers pinned to the mattress, his other urging her leg to ride higher upon his hip, opening her even more for the taking.

The pleasure spiked and receded until Theodore seemed to realize she needed something more. Something erotic and sure. Releasing her hands, he moved to a position that placed him on his haunches.

"Put both your hands on your breasts, love. Imagine I am touching you there and don't move them unless I say," he instructed darkly. When she hesitated, his brow rose high as if daring her to defy him.

Shyly, she did as he asked, splaying her fingers across the white flesh, her pink nipples peeking through. Theodore's eyes closed for a moment as if the sight was more than he could bear, then he pinned her with a stare so full of emotion, Lauren felt it in her very bones.

"You are so goddamn beautiful," he muttered.

Rolling his hips in the most wicked of fashions, he reared back and reached between her thighs where their bodies were joined.

A steady forefinger and thumb tweaked the button of nerves, and Lauren cried out loud. It felt too good, too raw and over-whelming. There was the pain of being filled by him, her heated flesh stretching and molding around him, then the lavish, sweetly agonizing beauty of his hand touching her, gliding, plucking, rubbing until she was on the verge of something unknown. A cliff of sorts that beckoned her to plunge over.

"Come for me, love," Theodore commanded, his eyes glittering fiercely as he watched her writhe helplessly below him. "Come for me now."

Lauren felt her body change in that moment, a startling transformation that should have frightened her rather than thrilled her. Her body, instead of instinctively rejecting his cock, surrendered at last, the tissues and internal muscles sucking at him so he could not withdraw.

The pain, still lurking there in the background, receded. Where his fingers played her, the sensations collided with the spot where his cock hit deep. Another deliberate rotation and plunge of his hips, a firmer press of his fingers, and everything merged and melted. An inferno of bliss and love and pleasure that sent Lauren flying over that cliff and through the heavens.

She barely heard Theodore's muffled shout of release as he climaxed moments later. The stunning beauty of it all was still too new as he thrust one last time inside her with a satisfied, hoarse groan.

He collapsed atop her, breathing heavily. It was a welcome weight, necessary to ground her because she was floating on waves of color, lost in a paradise she never wanted to leave.

"Mine," he whispered in her ear. "Mine at last. My heart. My love. My life." He sought and found her lips.

Lauren smiled. "Mine."

SOMETIME LATER, Theodore stirred.

Rising from the bed, he located a soft cloth, dipped it in cool water, and set about cleansing the blood and fluid from Lauren's thighs. She squirmed a bit, embarrassed by the attention, but a few soothing words settled her. Relaxing against the pillows, she allowed him to do as he wished, and when he was done, she watched as he tossed the cloth into the fire so it would burn away.

Once back at her side, he gathered her close, tucking her beneath his arm, her head under his chin. When her arm wrapped around his waist, he felt his heart swell until he thought it might burst from his chest.

"I remember the first moment I saw you." The rumble of his words stirred her silky brown hair, and he tucked a stray strand of it behind her delicate ear. "I did not even know your name, had not the faintest idea who your family was, but I said to myself, that is the girl I will marry. I fell in love with you that very moment."

Lauren snuggled closer. "At the Clarita Musicale."

"Yes. You were standing on the garden terrace. It was before Lady Monica began playing, and you were consoling a child. Lady Monica's little sister, I believe it was."

"Lillith. She'd dropped her doll, and the porcelain head broke on the tiles. Poor dear was inconsolable." Lauren frowned at the remembrance. "Lady Monica accused her of dropping the doll on purpose to gain attention. Said she was a baby for bringing the doll to a musicale in the first place. Then Lady Monica stomped her foot and stormed off, calling for a servant to clean up the mess while poor little Lillith stood there, bewildered and embarrassed."

"You hurried over to her, bent down, and spoke gently to her while picking up the pieces before a servant came. By the end, you had coaxed a smile from her and dried her tears. Then you didn't even blink an eye when the girl insisted on sitting beside you with Lady Monica glaring at you the entire time she played her piece."

"You remember all of that?" Lauren leaned back, looking at him in surprise.

"Of course, I do. I told you I fell in love with you the first time I saw you. It stands to reason I would remember every detail of the occasion. You wore a powder blue gown with white lace trim, and when we were introduced, I thought your eyes were the shade of moonstones. Grey and silver bright. You were the most gorgeous creature I'd ever laid eyes upon. Still are."

"I barely recall our meeting," Lauren teased.

"Liar," Theodore breathed against her hair. "You could not hide your interest in me, either."

"It's true. When you began your pursuit of me, I was so happy." She hugged him tightly. "I'm sorry we wasted so much time apart. But never again."

Theodore pulled her up until she was sprawled across his chest and they were eye to eye. "Never again," he agreed, burying his hands in her hair and cradling her face. "Nothing will keep us apart from this moment on. I plan on marrying you as quickly as possible to make sure that is a reality."

CHAPTER 19

"We shall wed in the chapel at Hawthorne Greene," Theodore told Lauren in the early morning hours as he delivered her safely to her room under the cover of darkness. "I'll leave today for London, collect my mother and yours, provided she is well enough to travel, and secure a special license enabling us to wed. There are also a few legalities I must handle with my barrister and your own."

Lauren stood on tiptoes and pressed a kiss to his cheek. "I still don't understand why I can't go with you."

Theodore grinned and tweaked her nose. "Reputations, love. I'm desperately trying to keep yours lily-white. Trust me on this."

"I do trust you, Theo, and I love you."

"Then be ready to say 'I do' when I see you in Kent."

THAT AFTERNOON, Settleton was abuzz over the news the Earl of Hawthorne and Lady Lauren Kendall had renewed their engagement and would be married within days.

"I'm so happy for you both, darling," Penelope embraced Lauren, "and so happy you gave Hawthorne another chance."

Lady Emma hugged her tight next. "This is so exciting. Although we've only just become friends, I'm honored you extended an invitation to visit you and Lord Hawthorne after you are settled. It is a kindness I never expected."

"As was your kindness to me," Lauren murmured.

"Scandal is not a game one should play unwittingly." Emma laughed. "I learned my lesson."

"As did I." Lauren's brow rose as Melanie approached the small group of women. The girl had taken the news quite sullenly. Even now, a distinct scowl marred her pretty face.

"I heard something earlier, Lady Lauren, and I hope you forgive my curiosity, but several gentlemen were discussing your impending nuptials."

Lauren stiffened. "Oh? I can't imagine they would find the subject to be very interesting."

"The need for haste is a peculiar development. But what is a Christmas house party without a bit of scandal attached?" Perching on the settee, Melanie fluffed her skirts. "It's said Hawthorne will purchase that new cotton factory in Leeds now that he will have the benefit of your considerable inheritance. He's had his eye on it for some time, but Lord Eastwood's interest has grown recently as well. Perhaps they'll enter a bidding war. Wouldn't that be exciting?"

"Do hush, Melanie." Penelope frowned at her cousin-in-law. "You create needless gossip."

"But we all know how eagerly men spend new funds once it is within hand, Penelope. It's no secret Hawthorne will now control her fortune. Much to many a man's dismay." Melanie tilted her head, narrowed eyes giving Lauren a thorough consideration. "You would have been quite popular this season, Lady Lauren. All the rage, but you're now off the marriage mart, so to speak. Of course, you could have enjoyed a bit of independence, too."

"Hawthorne intends to set my monies aside," Lauren replied stiffly. "It is to be used at my own discretion. He'll not touch it."

Several of the ladies, noticeably uncomfortable in light of Melanie's obvious jealousy, now appeared shocked by Lauren's bold declaration. Even Penelope nervously tugged at Lauren's elbow, but she was determined to defend her future husband.

Melanie's eyes widened before she began laughing. "Oh, my dear! How droll you are with your stories." She smirked. "Surely, you don't believe that. It is unheard of, you know."

Lauren's chin rose stubbornly, although inwardly, her stomach clenched at the thought she'd fallen into a trap of her own making. Had she allowed love to blind her yet again? Or was she correct in placing all of her trust and love in Theodore? He mentioned the need to visit their barristers upon his arrival in London. To put in place the terms of the contract their fathers devised, perhaps. Or finalize the purchase of a cotton mill with newly obtained funds?

Nausea rose in Lauren's throat as she remembered their sweet kiss upon parting that very morning. He'd made no mention of his plans for her inheritance—not during the dark of night after making love to her, nor while they lay awake and whispered of their future together. She hadn't asked him either, too caught up in the magic of being his to consider he might have used her.

"Maybe I am naïve, but I've faith the earl will do as he says. I've no reason not to believe him." Lauren's tone was firm, but Melanie, sensing weakness, snatched that opportunity to press the point.

"But you can't be sure, and once you are wed, it's unfortunately too late. Everything you have becomes his, including yourself." Finally, heeding Penelope's burning glare, Melanie shrugged and offered Lauren an insincere smile. "Despite all that, I do extend my felicitations. I'm sure Hawthorne is pleased with the way things turned out. It is to his benefit, after all. The mere suggestion a woman should have charge of her own funds is something men aren't likely to ever embrace. It's foolish, but a pleasant dream for some, I suppose."

~

TWO DAYS PASSED QUICKLY, and the weather cooperated with bright sunshine, although it remained frigid enough that the snow stayed intact.

Lauren alternated between very different emotions—dizzying happiness that she would soon become Theodore's wife, and nagging despair she was possibly barreling headlong into the biggest mistake of her life.

Anne spent the time bustling about, packing Lauren's belongings with cheerful enthusiasm and sighing over the romanticism of the impending elopement. If she worried over her mistress's change of heart regarding marriage in general, she kept those thoughts private.

Lauren stood in the foyer and bid Penelope and George goodbye. Everyone had come down to see her off, and the well-wishes did much to lift her spirits. Even Lord Sanderson, who'd carefully avoided her, bowed over her hand and wished her and the earl much happiness. Of course, it did not escape notice that he just briefly touched her, and only because courtesy dictated it. No doubt, Theodore's warning still echoed in the man's ears.

"Goodbye, dear cousin. Remind Hawthorne of our plans to visit you both before the Season begins." George kissed Lauren on the cheek, and Penelope did the same.

"Yes. Now that he will be relations, he should expect to see more of us. It shall make for merry holidays in the future. Especially once children begin appearing. Oh! Imagine the fun we shall have then!"

Lauren blushed hotly. "Penelope! We've not even wed yet, and here you speak of children."

Penelope winked at her. "It's never too early to speak of starting a family, dear cousin." Her hand slid to her own stomach, and Lauren understood her meaning. "They bring so much magic to ordinary life."

Lauren hugged Penelope fiercely while George gave them a suspicious glance. "Take good care of yourself, and I will see you both soon. And you as well, Lady Emma."

Climbing into the coach with Ollie's assistance, Lauren waved through the glass at everyone gathered to see her off while Anne settled the warming pot at their feet.

"On to Hawthorne Green, my lady, and your new life as a countess," Anne said excitedly.

Lauren chewed her bottom lip as the coach lurched forward. From the train station, it was a relatively short trip to Kent where Theodore's family estate was located.

Their marriage would take place, and hopefully, a betrayal of her heart would not materialize.

THE AFTERNOON WAS SURPRISINGLY WARM, and the garden, although starkly bare, contained a few splashes of color from blooming winter roses. Lauren lifted her face to the sun, savoring the balminess.

She'd left the Gold Parlor after taking tea with her mother and Lady Hawthorne. The two older ladies had only arrived together just the day before, and although it was a very sweet reunion, Lauren was bitterly disappointed Theodore was not with them.

"Some business matter that needed attending, my dear," his mother had said with a wave of her hand. "Theodore assured us he will arrive by tomorrow."

Lady Katherine Kendall had given her daughter a hug. "I'm grateful I felt well enough to travel. When Lord Hawthorne arrived to tell me the news, I was almost as excited as he." Tucking a stray lock behind Lauren's ear, her mother gave her a tender smile. "I cannot tell you how happy I am you renewed your relationship with the earl. Your happiness is of the utmost importance to him, Lauren, and to me."

Lady Hawthorne bustled in closer, fighting back a sniffle. "Oh, dear. Now, I believe that I may cry from sheer joy."

"No tears until the wedding, Louisa," Katherine admonished gently. "Lauren is already nervous, and besides, I'm not sure she's completely forgiven either of us for our subterfuge in bringing her and Hawthorne back together. Isn't that right, darling?"

"Of course, I've forgiven you. Theodore and I are in love, so our marriage is a logical conclusion," Lauren replied, slipping an arm around the waist of both women. "Neither of us desire a longer engagement when there is little purpose for it. I hope Theodore concludes his business quickly and returns to us safely."

Remembering the conversation now, Lauren felt that odd pang in her chest again. She did not know what the business matter could be, but she suspected it involved the factory Theodore wished to purchase. Although it was just as likely to be the procurement of the special license enabling their hasty marriage.

Oh, it will drive me mad thinking about it, so I must stop.

"Yes, I will stop thinking about it," she muttered aloud to the sky, eyes closed as a light breeze drifted over her face and a cloud darkened the sun's rays for a brief moment.

"What is it you will not think about, my love? Tell me, for I've thought of nothing but you for days and days, and the sun refused to shine until this moment." Theodore brushed a soft kiss across her lips.

Lauren's eyes fluttered open to see him silhouetted against the brilliant blue sky.

Her heart quivered wildly. Theodore was here. He came for her. To marry her and make her his. A small moan worked its way up her throat.

"You've come," she managed to say as he remained bent over, blocking the sun as his mouth hovering above hers.

"Of course, I came. My entire world is waiting right here." Theo rubbed his thumb over her lips then down to the hollow of her throat and the tiny patch of skin exposed by the cloak she wore against the occasional chilly breeze. "As beautiful and delicate as those winter roses and just as precious." He tested the pulse beating erratically just below the surface of her skin and frowned. "Did you doubt my commitment?"

"No, Theo. I only thought you would arrive sooner. I-I missed you."

He smiled down at her. "And I missed you. I stopped in the village and made arrangements with Reverend Hapstone. Our wedding will take place in the morning. Does this please you?" Taking her by the elbows, Theo pulled Lauren to her feet. "It was either that or wait until after Christmas. I cannot wait any longer, for you see, I'm horribly impatient."

"Yes," she said, wrapping her arms around his waist. With her face pressed against his overcoat, she breathed in his scent. It was crafted of sandalwood and leather, a touch of juniper perhaps. Utterly delicious and tempting. The heat of his body leached through their clothes to warm her as he engulfed her in his embrace.

"You are melancholy for some reason. What is it, darling?" Theodore whispered against her ear.

Lauren sucked in a breath and held it. How could she tell him she worried he was getting his way with the use of her inheritance? How could she explain her insecurities when it came to such things? Especially when she had buried them so deep after witnessing her mother's happiness and Lady Hawthorne's excitement over the impending marriage. She would look a fool if she brought it up now.

"It is nothing, Theo. Just nerves, I suppose. Do our mothers know you've arrived? They will be so happy knowing you are finally here."

Theodore pulled away, staring down at her with a tilt of his head. "We won't start our marriage with a lie, Lauren. We've promised ourselves that, remember?" His eyes, the color of the brilliant blue sky, darkened. "Now, tell me what is the matter. Did something happen at your cousin's? You were not insulted, I hope?"

Lauren sank back down on the bench, and after a moment, Theodore sat beside her. The question she most wanted answered bubbled inside her to the time of Lady Melanie's vengeful voice. While she wanted to shake her head to clear the doubts away, for they clung like spiderwebs, her pulse thumped furiously with apprehension to hear his answer.

Truthfully? She did not want to know his answer. It would hurt too much.

"Did you purchase a cotton factory while in London?" she abruptly blurted out.

Theodore's expression registered surprise before hardening into one of agitation. "I see the gossips could not help themselves."

Stomach roiling with sudden nausea, Lauren considered that answer.

Because it was not a denial.

"You did, and you used my inheritance." Her voice came out soft and sad. Dizzy with realization, she shot to her feet. "How could you do this to me? How could you use me so callously after I gave you my heart? My... my soul."

Theodore yanked her back down to the bench, his chin clenched tight with annoyance. With the pressure of a steel trap, his fingers wrapped around her elbow and held her hostage. "You know I would not do that, Lauren. Not after what we've been through. Not after our fathers tried using us both to further their own agendas."

With his free hand, he rifled through his overcoat pockets, searching for something while still keeping his grip tight on her elbow.

"Contrary to popular thought, I did not purchase a cotton factory. I did, however, enter into an agreement upon it with a contingency in place. It depends on whether you would like me to purchase it for you—with my funds. Not a shilling of yours would be used. Of course, today's archaic laws being what they are, I must do things this way before placing the title in your name. But it's a damn fine investment. Not to mention, it could be managed in a proper, humane way if someone honorable was in charge of things." His words came out in a growl. "I told you before, Lauren. I won't ever use your inheritance for my own gain. It is yours. Yours alone. Our barristers drew up the proper documents yesterday, placing all your money in a separate account under your name upon our marriage."

He withdrew three folded sheets of vellum from an inner coat pocket, the gold seals gleaming in the sunlight as he handed them to her.

One was the special license for their marriage, one was an agreement to purchase the cotton factory in Leeds with the title to be placed in her married name upon her approval of the transaction, and the third was a document placing all inheritance funds into a special account only she had access to.

There was silence as Lauren gathered the documents in hand. She keenly felt Theodore's disappointment. His indignation at his honor being questioned pricked at her heart, and shame for her reactions to another's jealous gossip sent a hot flush of scarlet across her cheeks.

"I'm sorry, Theodore," she said simply.

Theodore's eyes were still that dark indigo shade. A muscle in his jaw ticked, a sure indicator he was upset with her lack of faith.

"I meant it to be a surprise," he explained gruffly." A sort of wedding gift, if you will."

There was nothing she could say, so she just nodded, drowning in misery that she'd upset him.

After a few uncomfortable minutes of silence, Theodore released her arm. Rising from the bench, he stood gazing down at her, his face now an inscrutable mask.

"I shall let our mothers know of my arrival and that the wedding shall occur in the morning. Place those documents somewhere safe."

With a quick pivot on his heel, Theodore left her there in the garden amongst the winter roses.

The breeze fanning her cheeks seemed chillier than any she'd felt all winter.

A repayment, perhaps, for her own betrayal.

CHAPTER 20

*I*t was done.

They were wed.

After attending the traditional wedding breakfast, they now fulfilled their social obligation by taking tea in the Gold Parlor with their mothers, Reverend Hapstone and his wife, and Hawthorne Green's closest neighbors, the elderly Earl and Countess of Dragmore.

Theodore lifted Lauren's hand, pressing a kiss to the back of it while she chewed the corner of her lip in a gesture he'd discovered long ago indicated overwhelming nervousness.

His new wife was uncharacteristically quiet, notwithstanding the fact she'd become the new Countess of Hawthorne two hours prior to this moment. When he released her, she again stared at the huge, teardrop-shaped sapphire ring on her left hand. It was the ring he should have placed on her finger months ago, and a possessive thrill shot through him knowing she was finally, legally his wife.

She'd not had much to say since their chat in the garden the day before. He found himself reluctant to speak of the incident as well, and at dinner the previous evening, they were both content to allow their mothers to carry the conversation.

Theodore could not honestly say he wasn't still angry. Lauren's rapid decline into a state of mistrusting his motives hurt more than he wanted to admit. Knowing she'd wanted to hide her suspicions bothered him even more. He had no wish for his wife to keep anything from him, and he never wanted her too frightened to question his motives or offer opinions if she had different views.

But then, he'd not handled things very well either. In the face of her sincere apology, he'd stormed off like a spoiled child when he could have accepted it, and then apologized in turn for not understanding how she might take the gossip swirling around their scandalous elopement.

He sighed heavily, snaking an arm around her waist. Lauren gave him a startled glance, excusing herself from the lively conversation their mothers were currently having on how best to break the news to the *ton.*

"Countess, if you would like a bit of privacy, we can retire to our chambers. The others will not mind. In fact, it is probably expected."

Lauren's eyes widened a little, and for a breath, Theodore thought she might refuse. She stood silent for a long moment, then shyly nodded in agreement.

Theodore wasted no time in making their excuses, and as they made their departure, a round of applause erupted. Lauren flushed such a blazing shade of red it was possible she might be in danger of passing out. Her bouquet, a mix of the red winter roses and bright green and white mistletoe, trembled in her hand. Was she frightened of being alone with him, or truly embarrassed by the attention from their guests?

Shaking his head at Anne, who waited outside the parlor ready to assist her mistress at a moment's notice, Theodore escorted Lauren to the base of the wide, curving staircase.

"I'll handle things from here, Anne. Thank you, though." He shot the maid a wink, which sent her into a blushing fit as well. "We'll ring for you later to bring up a light meal."

Lauren did not say a word, merely pressed her lips tighter and allowed Theodore to lead her up the marble stair treads. Once they reached his suite of rooms, Theodore tossed off his formal coat and raked a hand through his chestnut hair.

He allowed his gaze to roam over his little bride. She stood in the middle of the largest room, appearing both fascinated and apprehensive.

Theodore's features softened. How he loved her. Even if she still mistrusted him, he still worshipped the ground she walked.

"You look so beautiful in that gown, Lauren. Stunning, in fact."

Her eyes fell to the bodice of the dress and the tiny seed pearls decorating the bodice. "Thank you. It is really my wedding dress, the one I was supposed to wear before. Mother brought it with her from London." Her fingers traced the lace trim of the veil in the coil of silky brown hair. Soft tendrils escaped the low chignon, teasing her neck and tempting his hands to stroke her skin. "The veil, too. I told her I did not need to wear it this morning, but she insisted."

"I'm glad she did. It is perfection on you." Theodore stepped closer, his forefinger grazing the line of her jaw and lifting her chin until she stared into his eyes. "May I help you disrobe?"

"Yes."

She stood, waiting for him to decide how he would proceed. Slowly walking around her, he placed a hand at the curve of her waist and swept the filmy tulle of the veil aside and over her shoulder.

The back of the silk, ivory-hued dress consisted of a row of buttons matching the pearls decorating the bodice. There appeared to be two hundred of the little devils, and Lord only knew how his suddenly clumsy fingers might accomplish this task.

But he managed.

She released a sigh when he was done unfastening them all, and Theodore held back a groan as the next layer of garments came into view through the opened back. A creamy confection of a corset emerged as he helped Lauren carefully step out of the puddle of skirts. Matching silk stockings and tiny, bow-topped heeled slippers completed the vision of loveliness. She still held her bouquet, so he removed it from her hand. Before tossing it aside, he plucked a piece of mistletoe from its center.

He twirled her slowly so she faced him, his palm easing down her side until it rested on her curved hip.

"Lauren."

The husky tone of his voice made her sway. Her eyes drifted shut then opened to lock on his. The grey shade of her irises was nearly obliterated by the darkness of the pupils, dilated as they were with arousal. He showed her the mistletoe, and her breath caught.

"A truth. I love you. You know that, don't you?"

"Yes, Theodore." She swallowed, her hands lifting so that she cradled his face in her palms. "A truth. I love you. More than you can possibly know. I'm sorry for doubting you again. Will you forgive me?"

He kissed her softly as he tossed the mistletoe aside. "I will always forgive you if you will always forgive me, for we are bound to make mistakes, and there will be misunderstandings. But I swear to you, I will never stop loving you."

"And I will never stop loving you." She sighed as he pulled at the strings of the corset, loosening them until the boned structure fell away, revealing a thin, silky chemise beneath. Suppressing a growl, Theodore drew that over her head, careful not to disturb the veil. For some reason, the thought of her body partially concealed by the dream-like material was highly erotic, as was the idea of her keeping on the stockings and delicate shoes.

"Now that you are my wife, you should know I plan on thoroughly corrupting you within the confines of our bedroom." He trailed a line of open-mouth kisses down her throat, scalding and persistent on the chosen path toward her breasts. Reaching one pale, pink tip, he sucked it deep into his mouth, groaning because she was as sweet as confectioner's sugar on his tongue.

"I would be thoroughly disappointed if you did not."

As she spoke, her hands tugged at his shirttails, pulling them free of his trousers before moving on to the button placket. After a few moments, Theodore tore himself away from suckling her breasts to quickly remove his garments. When Lauren moved to remove her veil and kick off her shoes, he stopped her, pulling her against the hard length of his body. She felt so good, his eyes closed against a wave of emotion.

"Leave them on, darling. You have no idea how gorgeous you are."

Scooping her up, he carried her to his bed, laying her down and arranging the veil so that it draped over her shoulders and flat belly.

"Beautiful." He kissed the soft skin under her bellybutton.

Lauren's hands smoothed over his wide shoulders. "Beautiful," she repeated.

When he settled his mouth against the flesh between her thighs, she arched into the heat of his tongue, an inarticulate cry escaping her lips. With a groan of absolute hunger, Theodore gripped her hips, holding her still for the lashing of his tongue as he drove her over the edge within a matter of minutes.

Kissing his way back up her body, he lavished attention to her breasts, licking and tugging them deep into his mouth before giving the hard buds a teasing nip from his sharp teeth. When she was writhing beneath him again, he chuckled and began ravishing her mouth. Sliding his tongue along hers, he plunged deep and slow until she was whimpering for more, her hands frantically pulling at his body so he would come inside her.

Reaching a hand down between them, Theodore swept two fingers along the slick folds of womanly flesh. With sly purpose, he brushed over her clitoris, laughing softly when she shuddered.

"So wet. Wet and ready for me to take you. Are you ready, darling wife?"

"Please, Theodore. Have mercy on me. Make me yours," she moaned, wrapping her arms around his neck and attempting to pull him down harder on top of her. "I need… more…"

"Yes, love. I know you do, and I will give you that and more —anything you ask of me." With a quick motion, Theodore flipped her onto her stomach, his arm anchoring under her belly and lifting so that her bottom was raised higher in the air.

She squealed with the abrupt motion, but as he instructed her on what he wanted, she obeyed with a tortured moan of anticipation. Braced on her knees, face pressed to the coverlet and the veil pooling over her bare back, she was quite a sight. When her arms extended out above her head, her fists gripping the bedclothes, Theodore knew he'd never seen a woman so damned beautiful.

Standing beside the bed, he moved so that he was between her thighs. Her sex glistening with need, a quivering sigh escaped her when he smoothed a hand over the twin globes of her bottom. Perfectly round, the color of cream, and smooth as silk, they called for his hands. To mark them. To soothe them.

He gave one side an experimental swat and was rewarded with a surprised cry that died off in what might be a strangled groan of pleasure. His cock jerked in response. He treated the other side to the same, and Lauren gripped the counterpane harder. Her hips circled before jutting back toward him.

"Wait, darling. I'm coming in. Open for me. Open."

Taking his cock in hand, Theodore rubbed himself over the exposed flesh of her sex, gratified when she rocked against him, murmuring incoherently. He thought about making them both wait—making them both suffer the delicious torment of delayed satisfaction, but he couldn't. Not when she made such intoxicating sounds of need. Not when she moved so wantonly. He was mad for her and she for him. He needed her. Now.

Sliding inside her heat was like coming home. It was everything. It was warmth. It was silk. It was love and comfort and a sense of belonging. It was Lauren. That was enough.

"Christ, Lauren. I'll never get enough you. Never." He began moving, going so deep he felt the cusp of her womb, his hands gripping her hips, holding her steady for his conquering. He took her pleasure, gave it back a hundred times over, and in return, exploded with ecstasy he would never deserve. He climaxed inside her just as she reached a pinnacle so pure, so sweet it left her sobbing with its beauty.

Theodore collapsed beside Lauren, embracing her so hard she might have found it difficult to breathe in the circle of his arms. Tears dampened his own cheeks.

"You are a gift, Lauren, and I'll spend the rest of my days thanking God for you."

THE CLOCK STRUCK MIDNIGHT, and Lauren lifted her head as the final chime died away, studying the features of the man she loved. In the dim light of the room, she saw the faint tracks where tears stained his cheeks. That she possessed the power to wring such emotion from this powerful man was frightening. That he held the same power over her was terrifying.

And beautiful.

His eyes fluttered open, the blue depths shadowed, but Lauren did not need to see within them to know how he felt.

"It's Christmas," she whispered, her heart swelling with love.

"Yes," Theodore replied, rolling so she was beneath him yet again, their mouths meeting over and over. "Let us celebrate with a kiss and a reminder, wife. I am yours, and you are mine. Forever."

THE END

ACKNOWLEDGMENTS

As always, thank you to my readers for allowing me to experience this amazing journey. Whenever I receive emails, reviews, or notes, I just can't believe how blessed I am. To write, and have others read those words and enjoy them, is a dream come true. So, thank you from the bottom of my heart.

Very special thanks to Cheryl Maddox for her awesome PA duties and doing all the stuff to keep me on track. I adore you!

Thank you to Dakota at Dragonfly Ink Graphic Design Services for the gorgeous cover.

I could not do this without my sweet husband, James, by my side. He's always supportive in helping me accomplish my dreams. I can count on him—through thick and thin!

Thanks to the family and friends I can't live without. I love you all.

Special thanks to my friends in the book world. Michelle and Cindi: I love you ladies so much. Your encouragement and support mean the world to me.

To my ARC team readers: your time and support are invaluable! I appreciate each and every one of you. You are an important part of my journey as an author, and I'm blessed to have you read my words.

About April Moran

April enjoys writing both historical and new adult romance with a generous splash of heat. When not penning tales of passion, she enjoys traveling with her husband, attending rock concerts with friends, and time spent with family. Brainstorming new storylines is best done while riding her horse or during long walks with her German Shepherd. A tumbler of good whiskey helps tie all the details together and brings her characters to life.

BOOKS2READ.COM
https://books2read.com/author/april-moran/subscribe/33016

VISIT APRIL'S WEBSITE
www.aprilmoranbooks.com

SIGN UP FOR NEWSLETTER AND UPDATES
http://bit.ly/AprilMoran_BookUpdates
April Moran Book Updates

STALK APRIL EVERYWHERE

https://www.facebook.com/groups/aprilshoneybees/

https://www.bookbub.com/profile/april-moran

https://www.instagram.com/aprilmoranbooks

https://www.goodreads.com/Author-AprilMoran

https://www.pinterest.com/aprilmoranbooks

https://www.tiktok.com/authoraprilmoran